BLACK LIBRARY
SAMPLER

BLACK LIBRARY
SAMPLER

Guy Haley, Gav Thorpe, Thomas Parrott,
Dan Abnett, Chris Wraight, Sandy Mitchell,
Rachel Harrison, Josh Reynolds, C L Werner,
William King, Cavan Scott & Tom Huddleston

BLACK LIBRARY

A BLACK LIBRARY PUBLICATION

Dawn of Fire: Avenging Son first published in 2020.
Indomitus first published in 2020.
Nexus first published in *Nexus & Other Stories* in 2020.
The Devastation of Baal first published in 2017.
Xenos first published in 2001.
Watchers of the Throne: The Emperor's Legion first published in 2017.
First and Only first published in 1999.
For the Emperor first published in 2003.
Honourbound first published in 2019.
Horus Rising first published in 2006.
Sacrosanct first published in *Sacrosanct & Other Stories* in 2018.
Trollslayer first published in 1999.
Attack of the Necron first published in 2019.
City of Lifestone first published in 2019.
This edition published in Great Britain in 2020 by
Black Library,
Games Workshop Ltd.,
Willow Road,
Nottingham, NG7 2WS, UK.

10 9 8 7 6 5 4 3 2 1

Produced by Games Workshop in Nottingham.
Cover illustrations by Igor Sid (*Soul Wars*), Paul Dainton (*Indomitus*),
Marc Lee (*Honourbound*) and Neil Roberts (*Horus Rising*).

A CIP record for this book is available from the British Library.

ISBN 13: 978-1-80026-007-8

See Black Library on the internet at

blacklibrary.com

Find out more about Games Workshop
and the worlds of Warhammer at

games-workshop.com

Printed and bound by CPI Group (UK) Ltd, Croydon, CR0 4YY

Dear reader,

Let's start by telling you who we are.

Black Library is the publishing division of Games Workshop and creates science fiction, fantasy, horror, crime and children's fiction all set within the fantastic worlds of Warhammer 40,000 and Warhammer Age of Sigmar. We've been publishing now for over twenty years, and in that time have created thousands of amazing stories enjoyed by millions around the world.

Now, we acknowledge that this wonderful and rich legacy can make it challenging for a new reader in terms of knowing where to start. But fear not, help is at hand!

Within this free book you will find sample chapters from a specially curated range of Black Library titles. These chapters serve as an excellent introduction to the worlds of Warhammer, as well as the principal factions and iconic characters that exist within them – perfect for anyone new to Black Library. At the end of each extract we've included a 'Your Next Read' page, making it easy for you to find out where to go next.

We hope you enjoy the contents of this book and wish you many happy years of Warhammer reading.

The Black Library team

CONTENTS

AVENGING SON

A DAWN OF FIRE NOVEL

GUY HALEY

CHAPTER ONE

THE SIEGE OF TERRA

MESSINIUS

KHORNE'S LEGIONS

'I was there at the Siege of Terra,' Vitrian Messinius would say in his later years.

'I was there…' he would add to himself, his words never meant for ears but his own. 'I was there the day the Imperium died.'

But that was yet to come.

'To the walls! To the walls! The enemy is coming!' Captain Messinius, as he was then, led his Space Marines across the Penitent's Square high up on the Lion's Gate. 'Another attack! Repel them! Send them back to the warp!'

Thousands of red-skinned monsters born of fear and sin scaled the outer ramparts, fury and murder incarnate. The mortals they faced quailed. It took the heart of a Space Marine to stand against them without fear, and the Angels of Death were in short supply.

'Another attack, move, move! To the walls!'

They came in the days after the Avenging Son returned, emerging from nothing, eight legions strong, bringing the bulk of their numbers to bear against the chief entrance to the Imperial Palace. A decapitation strike like no other, and it came perilously close to success.

Messinius' Space Marines ran to the parapet edging the Penitent's Square. On many worlds, the square would have been a plaza fit to adorn the centre of any great city. Not on Terra. On the immensity of the Lion's Gate, it was nothing, one of hundreds of similarly huge spaces. The word 'gate' did not suit the scale of the cityscape. The Lion's Gate's bulk marched up into the sky, step by titanic step, until it rose far higher than the mountains it had supplanted. The gate had been built by the Emperor Himself, they said. Myths detailed the improbable supernatural feats required to raise it. They were lies, all of them, and belittled the true effort needed to build such an edifice. Though the Lion's Gate was made to His design and by His command, the soaring monument had been constructed by mortals, with mortal hands and mortal tools. Messinius wished that had been remembered. For men to build this was far more impressive than any godly act of creation. If men could remember that, he believed, then perhaps they would remember their own strength.

The uncanny may not have built the gate, but it threatened to bring it down. Messinius looked over the rampart lip, down to the lower levels thousands of feet below and the spread of the Anterior Barbican.

Upon the stepped fortifications of the Lion's Gate was armour of every colour and the blood of every loyal primarch. Dozens of regiments stood alongside them. Aircraft filled the sky. Guns boomed from every quarter. In the churning redness on the great roads, processional ways so huge they were akin to prairies cast in rockcrete, were flashes of gold where the Emperor's Custodian Guard battled. The might of the Imperium was gathered there, in the palace where He dwelt.

There seemed moments on that day when it might not be enough.

The outer ramparts were carpeted in red bodies that writhed and heaved, obscuring the great statues adorning the defences and covering over the guns, an invasive cancer consuming reality. The enemy were legion. There were too many foes to defeat by plan and ruse. Only guns, and will, would see the day won, but the defenders were so pitifully few.

Messinius called a wordless halt, clenched fist raised, seeking the best place to deploy his mixed company, veterans all of the Terran Crusade. Gunships and fighters sped overhead, unleashing deadly light and streams of bombs into the packed daemonic masses. There were innumerable cannons crammed onto the gate, and they all fired, rippling the structure with false earthquakes. Soon the many ships and orbital defences of Terra would add their guns, targeting the very world they were meant to guard, but the attack had come so suddenly; as yet they had had no time to react.

The noise was horrendous. Messinius' audio dampers were at maximum and still the roar of ordnance stung his ears. Those humans that survived today would be rendered deaf. But he would have welcomed more guns, and louder still, for all the defensive fury of the assailed palace could not drown out the hideous noise of the daemons – their sighing hisses, a billion serpents strong, and chittering, screaming wails. It was not only heard but sensed within the soul, the realms of spirit and of matter were so intertwined. Messinius' being would be forever stained by it.

Tactical information scrolled down his helmplate, near environs only. He had little strategic overview of the situation. The vox-channels were choked with a hellish screaming that made communication impossible. The noosphere was disrupted by etheric backwash spilling from the immaterial rifts the daemons poured through. Messinius was used to operating on his own. Small-scale, surgical actions were the way of the Adeptus Astartes, but in a battle of this scale, a lack of central coordination would lead inevitably to defeat. This was not like the first Siege, where his kind had fought in Legions.

He called up a company-wide vox-cast and spoke to his warriors. They were not his Chapter-kin, but they would listen. The primarch himself had commanded that they do so.

'Reinforce the mortals,' he said. 'Their morale is wavering. Position yourselves every fifty yards. Cover the whole of the south-facing front. Let them see you.' He directed his warriors by chopping at the air with his left hand. His right, bearing an inactive power fist, hung heavily at his side. 'Assault Squad Antiocles, back forty yards, single firing line. Prepare to engage enemy breakthroughs only on my mark. Devastators, split to demi-squads and take up high ground, sergeant and sub-squad prime's discretion as to positioning and target. Remember our objective, heavy infliction of casualties. We kill as many as we can, we retreat, then hold at the Penitent's Arch until further notice. Command squad, with me.'

Command squad was too grand a title for the mismatched crew Messinius had gathered around himself. His own officers were light years away, if they still lived.

'Doveskamor, Tidominus,' he said to the two Aurora Marines with him. 'Take the left.'

'Yes, captain,' they voxed, and jogged away, their green armour glinting orange in the hell-light of the invasion.

The rest of his scratch squad was comprised of a communications specialist from the Death Spectres, an Omega Marine with a penchant for plasma weaponry, and a Raptor holding an ancient standard he'd taken from a dusty display.

'Why did you take that, Brother Kryvesh?' Messinius asked, as they moved forward.

'The palace is full of such relics,' said the Raptor. 'It seems only right to put them to use. No one else wanted it.'

Messinius stared at him.

'What? If the gate falls, we'll have more to worry about than my minor indiscretion. It'll be good for morale.'

The squads were splitting to join the standard humans. Such was the noise many of the men on the wall had not noticed their arrival, and a ripple of surprise went along the line as they appeared at their sides. Messinius was glad to see they seemed more firm when they turned their eyes back outwards.

'Anzigus,' he said to the Death Spectre. 'Hold back, facilitate communication within the company. Maximum signal gain. This interference will only get worse. See if you can get us patched in to wider theatre command. I'll take a hardline if you can find one.'

'Yes, captain,' said Anzigus. He bowed a helm that was bulbous with additional equipment. He already had the access flap of the bulky vox-unit on his arm open. He withdrew, the aerials on his power plant extending. He headed towards a systems nexus on the far wall of the plaza, where soaring buttresses pushed back against the immense weight bearing down upon them.

Messinius watched him go. He knew next to nothing about Anzigus. He spoke little, and when he did, his voice was funereal. His Chapter was mysterious, but the same lack of familiarity held true for many of these warriors, thrown together by miraculous events. Over their years lost wandering in the warp, Messinius had come to see some as friends as well as comrades, others he hardly knew, and none he knew so well as his own Chapter brothers. But they would stand together. They were Space Marines. They had fought by the returned primarch's side, and in that they shared a bond. They would not stint in their duty now.

Messinius chose a spot on the wall, directing his other veterans to left and right. Kryvesh he sent to the mortal officer's side. He looked down again, out past the enemy and over the outer palace. Spires stretched away in every direction. Smoke rose from all over the landscape. Some of it was new, the work of the daemon horde, but Terra had been burning for weeks. The Astronomican had failed. The galaxy was split in two. Behind them in the sky turned the great palace gyre, its deep eye marking out the throne room of the Emperor Himself.

'Sir!' A member of the Palatine Guard shouted over the din. He pointed downwards, to the left. Messinius followed his wavering finger. Three hundred feet below, daemons were climbing. They came upwards in a triangle tipped by a brute with a double rack of horns. It clambered hand over hand, far faster than should be possible, flying upwards, as if it touched the side of the towering gate only as a concession to reality. A Space Marine with claw locks could not have climbed that fast.

'Soldiers of the Imperium! The enemy is upon us!'

He looked to the mortals. Their faces were blanched with fear. Their weapons shook. Their bravery was commendable nonetheless. Not one of them attempted to run, though a wave of terror preceded the unnatural things clambering up towards them.

'We shall not turn away from our duty, no matter how fearful the foe, or how dire our fates may be,' he said. 'Behind us is the Sanctum of the Emperor Himself. As He has watched over you, now it is your turn to stand in guardianship over Him.'

The creatures were drawing closer. Through a sliding, magnified window on his display, Messinius looked into the yellow and cunning eyes of their leader. A long tongue lolled permanently from the thing's mouth, licking at the wall, tasting the terror of the beings it protected.

Boltgun actions clicked. His men leaned over the parapet, towering over the mortals as the Lion's Gate towered over the Ultimate Wall. A wealth of targeting data was exchanged, warrior to warrior, as each chose a unique mark. No bolt would be wasted in the opening fusillade. They could hear the creatures' individual shrieks and growls, all wordless, but their meaning was clear: blood, blood, blood. Blood and skulls.

Messinius sneered at them. He ignited his power fist with a swift jerk. He always preferred the visceral thrill of manual activation. Motors came to full life. Lightning crackled around it. He aimed downwards with his bolt pistol. A reticule danced over diabolical faces, each a copy of all the others. These things were not real. They were not alive. They were projections of a false god. The Librarian Atramo had named them maladies. A spiritual sickness wearing ersatz flesh.

He reminded himself to be wary. Contempt was as thick as any armour, but these things were deadly, for all their unreality.

He knew. He had fought the Neverborn many times before.

'While He lives,' Messinius shouted, boosting his voxmitter gain to maximal, 'we stand!'

'For He of Terra!' the humans shouted, their battle cry loud enough to be heard over the booming of guns.

'For He of Terra,' said Messinius. 'Fire!' he shouted.

The Space Marines fired first. Boltguns spoke, spitting spikes of rocket flare into the foe. Bolts slammed into daemon bodies, bursting them apart. Black viscera exploded away. Black ichor showered those coming after. The daemons' false souls screamed back whence they came, though their bones and offal tumbled down like those of any truly living foe.

Las-beams speared next, and the space between the wall top and the scaling party filled with violence. The daemons were unnaturally resilient, protected from death by the energies of the warp, and though many were felled, others weathered the fire, and clambered up still, unharmed and uncaring of their dead. Messinius no longer needed his helm's magnification to see into the daemon champion's eyes. It stared at him, its smile a promise of death. The terror that preceded them was replaced by the urge to violence, and that gripped them all, foe and friend. The baseline humans began to lose their discipline. A man turned and shot his comrade, and was shot down in turn. Kryvesh banged the foot of his borrowed banner and called them back into line. Elsewhere, his warriors sang; not their Chapter warsongs, but battle hymns known to all. Wavering human voices joined them. The feelings of violence abated, just enough.

Then the things were over the parapet and on them. Messinius saw Tidominus carried down by a group of daemons, his unit signum replaced by a mortis rune in his helm. The enemy champion was racing at him. Messinius emptied his bolt pistol into its face, blowing half of it away into a fine mist of daemonic ichor. Still it leapt, hurling itself twenty feet over the parapet. Messinius fell back, keeping the creature in sight, targeting skating over his helmplate as the machine-spirit tried to maintain a target lock. Threat indicators trilled, shifting up their priority spectrum.

The daemon held up its enormous gnarled hands. Smoke whirled in the space between, coalescing into a two-handed sword almost as tall as Messinius. By the time its hoofed feet cracked the paving slabs of the square, the creature's weapon was solid. Vapour streaming from its ruined face, it pointed the broadsword at Messinius and hissed a wordless challenge.

'Accepted,' said Messinius, and moved in to attack.

The creature was fast, and punishingly strong. Messinius parried its first strike with an outward push of his palm, fingers spread. Energy crackled. The boom generated by the meeting of human technology and the sorceries of the warp was loud enough to out-compete the guns, but though the impact sent pain lancing up Messinius' arm, the daemon was not staggered, and pressed in a follow-up attack, swinging the massive sword around its head as if it weighed nothing.

Messinius countered more aggressively this time, punching in to the strike. Another thunderous detonation. Disruption fields shattered matter, but the daemon was not wholly real, and the effect upon it was lesser than it would be upon a natural foe. Nevertheless, this time it was thrown backwards by the blow. Smoke poured from the edge of its blade. It licked black blood from its arm and snarled. Messinius was ready when it leapt: opening his fist, ignoring the sword as it clashed against his pauldron and sheared off a peeling of ceramite, he grabbed the beast about its middle.

The Bloodletters of Khorne were rangy things, all bone and ropey muscle, no space within them for organs. The false god of war had no need for them to eat or breathe, or to give the semblance of being able to do so. They were made only to kill, and to strike fear in the hearts of those they faced. Their waists were solid, and slender, and easily encompassed by Messinius' power fist. It squirmed in his grip, throwing Messinius' arm about. Servo motors in his joints locked, supplementary muscle fibres strained, but the White Consul stood firm.

'Tell your master he is not welcome on Terra,' he said. His words were calm, a deliberate defiance of the waves of rage pulsing off the daemon.

He closed his hand.

The daemon's midriff exploded. The top half fell down, still hissing and thrashing. Its sword clanged off the paving and broke into shards, brittle now it was separated from its wielder. They were pieces of the same thing, sword and beast. Apart, the weapon could not survive long.

Messinius cast down the lower portion of the daemon. There were dozens of the things atop the wall, battling with his warriors and the human soldiery. In the second he paused he saw Doveskamor hacked down as he stood over the body of his brother, pieces of armour bouncing across the ground. He saw a group of Palatine Sentinels corner a daemon with their bayonets. He saw a dozen humans cut down by eldritch swords.

Where the humans kept their distance, their ranged weapons took a toll upon the Neverborn. Where the daemons got among them, they triumphed more often than not, even against his Space Marines. Support fire rained down sporadically from above, its usefulness restricted by the difficulty of picking targets from the swirling melee. At the western edge of the line, the heavy weapons were more telling, knocking daemons off the wall before they crested the parapet and preventing them from circling around the back of the

Imperial forces. Only his equipment allowed Messinius to see this. Without the helm feeds of his warriors and the limited access he had to the Lion Gate's auspectoria, he would have been blind, lost in the immediate clash of arms and sprays of blood. He would have remained where he was, fighting. He would not have seen that there were more groups of daemons pouring upwards. He would not have given his order, and then he would have died.

'Squad Antiocles, engage,' he said. He smashed a charging daemon into fragments, yanked another back the instant before it gutted a mortal soldier, and stamped its skull flat, while switching again to his company vox-net. 'All units, fall back to the Penitent's Arch. Take the mortals with you.'

His assault squad fell from the sky on burning jets, kicking daemons down and shooting them with their plasma and bolt pistols. A roar of promethium from a flamer blasted three bloodletters to ash.

'Fall back! Fall back!' Messinius commanded, his words beating time with his blows. 'Assault Squad Antiocles to cover. Devastators maintain overhead fire.'

Squad Antiocles drove the enemy back. Tactical Space Marines were retreating from the parapet, dragging human soldiers with them. An Ultramarine walked backwards past him, firing his bolter one-handed, a wounded member of the Palatine Guard draped over his right shoulder.

'Fall back! Fall back!' Messinius roared. He grabbed a human by the arm and yanked him hard away from the monster trying to slay him, almost throwing him across the square. He pivoted and punched, slamming the man's opponent in the face with a crackling bang that catapulted its broken corpse over the wall edge. 'Fall back!'

Mortal soldiers broke and ran while Squad Antiocles held

off the foe. Telling to begin with, in moments the assault squad's momentum was broken, and again more bloodletters were leaping over the edge of the rampart. The Space Marines fired in retreat, covering each other in pairs as they crossed the square diagonally to the Penitent's Arch. The mortals were getting the idea, running between the Adeptus Astartes and mostly staying out of their fire corridor. With the fight now concentrated around Squad Antiocles, the Devastators were more effective, blasting down the daemons before they could bring their weight of numbers to bear upon Antiocles. Sporadic bursts of fire from the retreating Tactical Marines added to the effect, and for a short period the number of daemons entering the square did not increase.

Messinius tarried a moment, rounding up more of the humans who were either too embattled or deaf to his orders to get out. He reached three still firing over the parapet's edge and pulled them away. A daemon reared over the parapet and he crushed its skull, but a second leapt up and cleaved hard into his fist, and power fled the weapon. Messinius pumped three bolts into its neck, decapitating it. He moved back.

His power fist was ruined. The daemon's cut had sliced right through the ceramite, breaking the power field generator and most of the weapon's strength-boosting apparatus, making it a dead weight. He said a quick thanks to the machine's departed spirit and smashed the top of his bolt pistol against the quick seal release, at the same time disengaging the power feeds by way of neural link. The clamps holding the power fist to his upper arm came loose and it slid to the floor with a clang, leaving his right arm clad in his standard ceramite gauntlet. A century together. A fine weapon. He had no time to mourn it.

'Fall back!' he shouted. 'Fall back to the Penitent's Arch!'

He slammed a fresh clip into his bolt pistol. Squad Antiocles were being pushed back. The Devastators walked their fire closer in to the combat. A heavy bolter blasted half a dozen daemons into stinking meat. A missile blew, lifting more into the air. Messinius fell back himself now, leaving it to the last moment before ordering the Assault Marines to leap from the fray. Their jets ignited, driving back the daemons with washes of flame, and they lifted up over his head, leaving four of their brothers dead on the ground. Devastator fire hammered down from above. Anti-personnel weapons set into casemates and swivel turrets on the walls joined in, but the daemons mounted higher and higher in a wave of red that flooded over the parapet.

'Run!' he shouted at the straggling human soldiery. 'Run and survive! Your service is not yet done!'

The Penitent's Arch led from the square onto a wall walk that curved around to another layer of defences. His Space Marines were already making a firing line across the entrance. A gate could be extended across the arch, sealing the walk from the square, but Messinius refrained from requesting it be closed, as the humans were still streaming past the Adeptus Astartes. Kryvesh waved the banner, whirling it through the air to attract the terrified mortals. The Space Marines fired constantly into the mass of daemons sprinting after them, exhausting their ammunition supplies. Shattered false bodies tumbled down, shot from the front and above, yet still they came, overtaking and dismembering the last warriors fleeing away from the parapet.

Squad Antiocles roared through the arch, landing behind their brethren. Messinius passed between them. For a moment he surveyed the tide of coming fury. Endless red-skinned monsters filling the square like a lake of spilled blood, washing over a score of brightly armoured Space Marine corpses left behind in the retreat. Several hundred humans lay alongside them.

He opened a vox-channel to Gate Command.

'Wall batteries three-seven-three through three-seven-six, target sector nine five eighty-three, Penitent's Square, western edge. Five-minute bombardment.'

'On whose order?'

'Captain Vitrian Messinius, White Consuls Chapter, Tenth Company. I have the primarch's authority.' As he dealt with gunnery control, he was also datapulsing a request for resupply, and checking through layered data screeds.

'Voice print and signum ident match. Transponder codes valid. We obey.'

The far side of the square erupted in a wall of flame. Heavy cannon shells detonated in a string along the rampart. High-energy beams sliced into the square, turning stone and metal instantly to superheated gas. The approaching daemons were annihilated. A few bolt-rounds cracked off as the last daemons nearing the Space Marine line were put down.

'Company, cease fire. Conserve ammunition.' Nobody heard him. Nobody could. He re-sent the order via vox-script. The boltguns cut out.

Penitent's Square was a cauldron of fire so intense he could feel the heat through his battleplate's ceramite. The ground shook under his feet and he considered the possibility that the wall would give way. The noise was so all-consuming the idea of speech lost relevance. For five minutes the Lion's Gate tore madly at its own hide, ripping out chunks of itself in a bid to scrape free the parasites infesting its fabric, then, as suddenly as it had begun, the bombardment ceased.

Where the Penitent's Square had been, a twisted mass

of black metal and shattered stone remained. So formidable were the defences of the Lion's Gate that the structure beneath had not been penetrated, but it was like this, in small bursts of destruction, that they could lose this war.

Messinius accessed the gate's noosphere. No daemons had as yet rounded the projecting Penitent's Spur to come up against their new position. When the attack came again, which it would, it would come from the front.

An ammunition train raced down the walkway from the fortress interior and came to a squealing stop fifty yards away. Medicae personnel jumped down. A Space Marine Apothecary came with them. Human peons rushed about with heavy sack bags full of bolter magazines, passing them out to the transhumans. Spent magazines clattered to the floor. New ones were slammed home. Messinius contacted his squad leaders, taking a quick census of his surviving men, not trusting the digits that read 'Company Casualties 23%' blinking in the upper right of his visual field.

Through the smoke given off by burning metal on the far side of the ruined square, he saw movement. Auspex returns tripped his armour's machine-spirit, and it blinked warnings in his helm.

<THREAT DETECTED.>

'They're coming again,' he said.

'My lord?' A soft voice, one that did not belong in that moment. He ignored it.

'Engage at fifty-yard range. Make every shot count.'

The ammunition train was hurriedly relieved of their allotted supplies, and sped off, bearing the worst-wounded, to aid whichever beleaguered unit needed it next.

'Stand ready.'

'My lord?' The voice became more insistent.

The voidships in orbit were beginning to fire. Their targeting systems were perturbed by the boiling warp energy and the vortex in constant motion over the Imperial Palace, and many shots went wide, crashing down into the Anterior Barbican, a few falling as far out as Magnifican.

Red monsters bounded towards them, as numerous as before, as if their efforts to thin them had been for naught.

'Fire,' he said coldly.

'My lord, your duty rotation begins in half an hour. You told me to wake you.'

This time he heard. Bolters boomed. Messinius froze them with a thought, and with another he shut down the hypnomat entirely.

Vitrian Messinius awoke groggily.

'My lord,' his servant said. Selwin, he was called. 'You are returned from your recollections?'

'I am awake, Selwin, yes,' Messinius said irritably. His mouth was dry. He wanted to be left alone.

'Shall I?' Selwin gestured to the hypnomat.

Messinius nodded and rubbed his face. It felt numb. Selwin flicked a number of toggles on the hypnomat and it powered down, the steady glow of its innards fading to nothing and winking out, taking the immediacy of Messinius' memories with it.

'The wall again?' Selwin asked.

The hypnomat's primary use was to instil knowledge without active learning on the subject's part, but it could reawaken memories to be lived again. Full immersion in the hypnomat required cooperation from Messinius' catalepsean node, and coming out of the half-sleep was never as easy as true waking. Reliving past events dulled his wits. Messinius reminded himself to be guarded. He forgot sometimes that he was not on Sabatine any more. The local saying 'This is Terra' encompassed a multitude of sins. Spying was among them.

'Yes,' he said. 'Personal debriefing.' He shook his head and unplugged the hypnomat's input cables from the neural ports set into his arms and neck. 'Nothing new learned.'

Selwin nodded, then hesitantly said, 'If I may be so bold as to ask, why do it, my lord, if you expect to learn nothing?'

'Because I can always be wrong,' Messinius said. He pointed at the hypnomat. It was a bulky machine set on a trolley, but not too big for an unaltered man to move. 'Take that away. Inform my armourer I will be with him in a few minutes.'

Selwin bowed. 'Already done, my lord.'

YOUR
NEXT READ

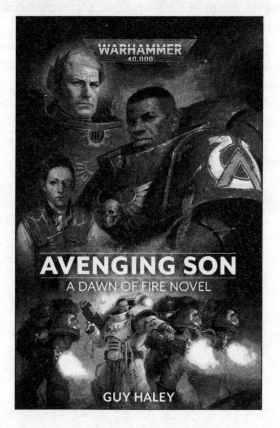

AVENGING SON
by Guy Haley

By the will of the reborn primarch Roboute Guilliman, the Indomitus Crusade spreads across the galaxy, bringing the Emperor's light back to the Dark Imperium. In the Machorta Sound, a desperate mission could determine the fate of the crusade – and battle is joined…

INDOMITUS

GAV THORPE

CHAPTER ONE

'They shall be pure of heart and strong of body, untainted by doubt and unsullied by self-aggrandisement.' Praxamedes had spoken without thought, the words of the Codex Astartes coming to him unbidden and reaching his tongue before he could stop them.

'Is that censure of a senior officer, Lieutenant Praxamedes?' asked Aeschelus as he looked away from the command bridge's main viewing display. The Ultramarines captain paced across the strategium of the *Ithraca's Vengeance*, heading to where his second-in-command stood alongside the task force's other lieutenant, Nemetus.

The polished blue of their armour danced with the amber-and-red glow of console lights, smudged by a bright plasma gleam shining from the tactical videolith that dominated the wall of the large command chamber. Tac-slaved servitors wired to terminals and augur banks grunted and chattered their dataflows to azure-robed overseers, who in turn compiled reports for their Space Marine officers. Behind them, Ship-master Oryk Oloris, in heavy trousers that were tucked into knee-high boots and a crisp white shirt beneath his Ultra-marines uniform tunic, prowled the deck with a watchful eye.

Praxamedes instantly regretted his momentary lapse.

'As a scholar of the lord primarch's teachings, you would know that the Codex Astartes has much to say on respect for the chain of command.' Aeschelus came alongside his two officers and half-turned back towards the main screen. He opened his hand towards the screen, indicating the star-ship that drifted across the spray of stars, plumes of blue and white plasma ejecting haphazardly from a ruptured reactor. 'Our preliminary surveyor reports indicate that we have dis-abled their weapons grid. The threat is minimal.'

'My words, brother-captain, were in reference to Nemetus' overly keen desire to lead the boarding,' Praxamedes told his superior. 'There are still enemy vessels in the vicinity.'

'Two destroyers,' scoffed Nemetus. 'Too fast a prey to hunt on our own. As soon as we give chase, they will disap-pear into the asteroids and gas clouds on the boundary of the third orbital sphere. Would you follow them into that, knowing that they could turn on us under the cover of our overwhelmed scanners?'

'That was not my suggestion, brother-lieutenant,' said Praxamedes, frowning. It was an occasional fault of Nem-etus to protest against an ill-thought strategy that had not, in fact, been raised, perhaps purely to show that he had considered and discarded such action himself. 'Our primary objective is destruction of the enemy. Boarding brings unnec-essary risk, at a time when the battle groups of Fleet Quintus must conserve their strength.'

'That is a Hellbringer-class cruiser,' added Nemetus. 'Nobody has built one for eight thousand years. It is a piece of archeo-tech in its own right.'

'The lord primarch would also favour heavily any intelligence we might glean from its cogitator banks,' said Aeschelus. 'We are at the forefront of the crusade, encountering foes fresh to the battle. This is a raider, an assault ship built for planetary attack. Perhaps this ship comes from beyond the Cicatrix Maledictum and could shed light on what is occurring in the Imperium Nihilus lost beyond the warp rifts.'

This time, Praxamedes was wise enough to hold his tongue, wishing the whole conversation would be forgotten. Aeschelus noticed his lieutenant's reticence and continued.

'You urge caution with a depleted resource, which is laudable, but I would not spend the lives of the lord primarch's warriors needlessly.' Aeschelus allowed his voice to travel a little further, carrying to other members of the command crew across the strategium. It was typical of Aeschelus' fine touch of command that he would turn potential remonstration into a moment to inspire others. It was a knack that Praxamedes sorely lacked, nor had any idea how to acquire despite his efforts.

'For near a decade, as ship-board chronometers reckon it, we have fought hard in the crusade of the lord primarch. At the outset there was treachery and catastrophe, losses suffered before the fleet had even left Terra. Our own task force lost its noble group master to the plague purges. Those here, and that came before, knew that there would be no easy victories, that a galaxy broken asunder by the witchery of our enemies would be an unwelcoming battlezone. Yet even the most pessimistic among us would not have countenanced the uncountable labours and obstacles that Fleet Quintus has found in its path.

'Every victory has been hard-fought and we have met with more reverses than those in other fleets. Each foe must be overcome in turn – every opportunity to rise from the shadows of past setbacks must be seized. Before us lies a prize, won by our own endeavour, that may lift the fortunes of not just the *Ithraca's Vengeance* or Battle Group Faustus, but perhaps bring heart to all of Crusade Fleet Quintus that our extraordinary travails have been to purpose.'

'A prize that is even now trying to slip from our fingers,' growled Nemetus, nodding towards the videolith. 'See how they crawl towards the stellar flotsam, seeking sanctuary in its midst. We must seize the moment, brother-captain.'

'And I stand ready to lead the attack, as always,' said Praxamedes. 'As the longest serving lieutenant it would be my honour to do so.'

'I have no doubt that you would be determined and diligent in the execution of the attack, Praxamedes, but I think this operation is more suited to the temperament of Nemetus.' The captain turned his full attention to the second lieutenant. 'Assemble your boarding force swiftly. Take control of the enemy strategium and extract what you can from the cogitators.'

'You'll need charges, to scuttle the ship when you are done,' said Praxamedes.

'There will be no need for that,' said Nemetus. 'It looks as though their reactors are already descending towards critical state. A few hours from now there will be nothing left but plasma.'

'All the more reason to fly swift and fight with narrow purpose,' said Aeschelus.

'If we're set on the mission, I'll review the augur data and calculate the approach vectors that will bring you most swiftly to your objective, brother.' Praxamedes lifted a fist to his chest to salute the departing officer.

Nemetus returned the gesture of respect with a nod. 'For the primarch and the Emperor.'

When the lieutenant had exited the strategium, Praxamedes turned to move towards the augur terminals. Aeschelus stopped him with a hand on his shoulder. He spoke quietly.

'I know that you think I undervalue you, Prax. I will give you battle command soon, I give you my word. It's just...'

'Nemetus is the more dynamic of us?'

'Restless,' Aeschelus replied. 'Nemetus excels in direct action. In all truth, would you have him providing overview for the expedition while you were leading the squads? Is that truly the best use of his and your aptitudes?'

Praxamedes said nothing. He had spoken out too much already and did not wish to push his superior's patience any further. In truth, he felt it was Aeschelus, in longing to prove his worth in the eyes of the primarch, that felt undervalued. Like many in the latest cohort of recruits pushed to the leading edges of the crusade, Aeschelus had not been in the fleet when those early disasters had occurred. He had not witnessed how the hope and excitement of the crusade's potential had withered in a matter of months.

Perhaps that was a good thing. Praxamedes had enough self-awareness to admit, to himself if no other, that those early experiences had given him a more pessimistic outlook than his new commander. The captain hoped Nemetus would bring glory to the *Ithraca's Vengeance* with some daring act, and Praxamedes was well aware of his own deficiencies in that regard. He was neither charismatic nor blessed with startling initiative. He was diligent and capable, and those were qualities that perhaps Battle Group Faustus needed right now when another serious setback might break the morale of the whole Fleet Quintus.

But Aeschelus was not interested in such thoughts and so Praxamedes kept them to himself.

'As you will it, brother-captain,' he said simply.

Aeschelus gave a nod of dismissal to set Praxamedes about his task, yet as the lieutenant moved away the captain felt the admonition in his formality. His second-in-command doubtless meant well but the last thing the command needed at the moment was negativity. There were finally reports of good news from the other battle groups, and while Faustus still laboured hard against warp storms and a ceaseless swarm of small but diverting traitor attacks, Aeschelus was determined that he would make a breakthrough soon.

Praxamedes tended to think in tactical terms, lacking the longer view of the strategic that had been inculcated into Aeschelus as part of his rapid training to the rank of captain. He and others like him had been despatched to the cutting edge of the Indomitus Crusade to bring some renewed urgency, particularly across Crusade Fleet Quintus.

Fresh blood, fresh energy.

Those had been the words of the lord primarch. Not heard in person, as Lord Guilliman was far from Terra leading the crusade when Aeschelus had been sent to his command. It wasn't like the days when Praxamedes and the first torchbearer fleets had been sent out. No fanfare, no primarch. Just reinforcements and a renewed will to press into the darkness.

One day, perhaps soon, Aeschelus would have the honour. One day he would stand before the lord primarch in victory, recognised for an effort that changed the fortunes of the fleet.

The captain broke from his reverie to find Oloris standing

close by, a dataslate in hand. The shipmaster raised a fist to his forehead.

'Latest fleet dispositions, captain.' The unaugmented human presented the dataslate and withdrew a step, brushing a wisp of blond hair from his pale face.

'Anything of note?' asked Aeschelus, knowing that Oloris could be trusted to review the information relevant to their current course of action.

'We received word that *Sword of Justice* and the *Vaputatian* both broke warp to rendezvous with the support fleet.'

'That leaves nobody on our starward flank. A little early for refit.' Aeschelus scrolled through the report but Oloris provided the answer first.

'They each had an unexpected encounter with a battleship-class enemy. They were able to break away but not before taking heavy damage.'

Aeschelus found the entry and accessed the engagement report. 'No identifier. Possible traitor flagship. Heavy lance arrays outranged our ships.'

'And us, captain,' said Oloris. He hesitated, cleared his throat and continued, 'Lieutenant Praxamedes wishes to know if we are proceeding with the boarding action.'

Aeschelus looked up. The lieutenant was at the augur console, ostensibly engaged in his preparations, though his enhanced hearing was more than capable of picking up the conversation between captain and shipmaster. It was protocol for any matters concerning the running of the vessel to come through the shipmaster, but it seemed peculiar on this occasion that Praxamedes had not delivered his question directly. It was likely that he was being more circumspect after his uncharacteristically outspoken moment.

'You have concerns, Prax?' the captain said, hoping informality would assure his subordinate that he was not in any way being censured. 'You think there is a danger presented by this rogue battleship?'

'It is a possibility, captain,' said Praxamedes, turning from his work. 'The engagement with the *Sword of Justice* took place within the last two days, only four hundred and fifty thousand miles from our current position. What if it's the Desolator?'

'I am surprised you put stock in such tales, lieutenant,' said Aeschelus. He snorted, shaking his head. 'The Desolator? Rumour and hearsay. The grumblings of reluctant Imperial Navy officers.'

'You think there is no truth to the reports, captain?' Praxamedes approached, darting a look towards Oloris that betrayed their conspiracy. 'Seven vessels lost or driven off in the last thirty days, all within this sub-sector.'

'There is no phantom enemy battleship striking with the speed of a frigate and disappearing.' Aeschelus raised a finger to forestall Oloris as the shipmaster opened his mouth to speak. 'And it certainly is not *The Ninth Eye*, that identification was based on the tiniest fragment of augur return and vox-scatter. Battle Group Command insist that there is no Alpha Legion presence in this whole sector. You want me to ignore the prize we have won based on the chattering of Navy officers?'

'I wished to clarify our intent, captain,' Praxamedes said stiffly. 'Your will is clear.'

'It is,' growled Aeschelus, now irritated by the lieutenant's intervention. 'Ready your calculations for Lieutenant Nemetus as quickly as possible.'

Aeschelus turned his eyes back to the drifting ship on the main display. This equivocation and rumour-mongering was just one of the many symptoms of the fleet's morale problems. He should not fault Praxamedes for falling prey to the same deficiencies as others caught up in the long tale of misfortune, but it was starting to affect his judgement. Despite his earlier words to the lieutenant, this kind of irrational behaviour, coupled with overfamiliarity to the non-Space Marine crew, made Aeschelus wonder if Praxamedes really was suited to any kind of battle command.

With the order for the boarding action given, the tone aboard the *Ithraca's Vengeance* changed from one of pensive watchfulness to energetic activity. The crews of the gun decks remained alert, sensor stations poring over the broken flank of the heavy cruiser, seeking any sign of sudden life from their foe. From the command bridge came firing solutions, pinpointing breaches in the enemy's armoured skin, selected to prepare the way for the incoming attack. In the flight bays the roar of plasma engines joined the thud of armoured boots, filling each launch deck with the noise of pending war. Red-clad tech-priests croaked and burbled sermons of the Machine-God to bless their charges before launch, lower adepts of the Cult of Mars anointing the gunships' weapons and targeting arrays with unguents while nano-laced censer smoke drifted into idling intakes to cleanse engine feeds.

Squad by squad, the boarding parties assembled at the mustering deck between the two flanking launch halls. Nemetus paced the concourse at the hall's centre, passing a critical eye over the thirty Space Marines as they came to attention. From the ship's complement he had selected three squads of Intercessors, the backbone of the new Primaris formations. Standing to attention, weapons presented, an unmoving line of Ultramarines blue, they awaited the order to break rank and move to board the gunships.

Unsullied by self-aggrandisement.

The words of Praxamedes lingered in the thoughts of Nemetus while he readied himself for the battle ahead. Whether intended for Aeschelus or Nemetus, that softly spoken line from the Codex Astartes had carried the same vehemence as a shouted outburst from any other. Praxamedes was calm to the point of coolness and guarded in everything he said. To have spoken as he did was almost without precedent.

Helmet under his arm, Nemetus walked along the ranks, inspecting every warrior. Each was impeccably turned out, a credit to themselves and the dedication of the armourium. Sergeant Villina lifted fist to chest as Nemetus reached the front of the formation once more.

'Most excellent, brother-sergeant, fit for a parade before the lord primarch himself!'

'And ready for more than just a parade, brother-lieutenant,' added the veteran sergeant.

'I am sure of it, Villina. It is my honour to lead them again.'

The Codex *Preparatory Statements on the Nature of the Adeptus Astartes* continued, and it was from the following words of the lord primarch that Nemetus took inspiration.

They will be bright stars on the firmament of battle, Angels of Death whose shining wings bring swift annihilation to the enemies of man.

A bright star in the firmament of battle.

Bright stars were in short supply of late, with the Imperium beset by all foes, both ancient and modern. A relative latecomer to the Indomitus Crusade, Nemetus had learned from afar of its great reconquest whilst undergoing his transformation and training. He knew the power of the stories

that returned from the exploits of humanity's finest warriors. He had heard temple bells ringing the triumphs of the
lord commander, listened to the cheers from hundreds of
thousands of throats as great victories were read from the
balcony-pulpits. As a Primaris Marine, he was to be the new
exemplar of everything the Adeptus Astartes represented.

And yet the words of Praxamedes still bit deep.

Unsettled, he passed an expert eye over the next warriors –
a squad of Eradicators, their melta rifles at the ready. They
would be the breaching team once the expedition reached
the enemy strategium. Nemetus' gaze moved between them
and the Intercessors, noting that most of their wargear was
freshly issued.

Many of Aeschelus' command had been sent as reinforcements
to Fleet Quintus, as had he and Nemetus; only a few were
longer-serving, having departed Terra at the crusade's outset.
Praxamedes was among those that had seen the earliest fighting, the most terrible wars and dogged campaigns. A member
of Fleet Quintus since its inception, he had risen from the
ranks while Nemetus and Aeschelus, and no few others, had
been trained to their officer roles. Such had been the early
casualties among the Space Marines – a force that lived by
the creed of leading from the front – that deaths among the
first Primaris officers had eliminated almost half the Adeptus
Astartes leadership of Fleet Quintus within three years. Battlefield promotions and brevet ranks were good as a stop-gap,
but as a longer term solution Nemetus and others had been
command-trained from the outset of their inductions.

Was Praxamedes' slight genuinely aimed at Aeschelus, a
subtle admonition for a superior who had been promoted
ahead of him?

That was an unkindness to Praxamedes, Nemetus decided.

The very moments before battle were not the best time to weigh up the motivations of his brother-officers, and Nemetus had nothing but respect for his fellow lieutenant. Praxamedes had simply been urging his usual circumspect approach, nothing more.

Nemetus turned his attention to the remaining members of his expedition. A little apart from the Intercessors stood ten Incursors, two combat squads of dedicated close assault specialists under Sergeant Dorium and Sergeant Lato. Clad in armour incorporating the most sophisticated internal auspex systems, they would pave the way for the main force, their bolt carbines ideally suited to the closer confines of the enemy starship. It had been just days since they had last seen action, and their wargear told a different story to that of the Intercessors. Here and there the lieutenant spied bare ceramite over some recently suffered damage, and the paint of their livery was much scratched.

'Is that blood?' Nemetus demanded, directing an accusing finger towards the gauntlet of Brother Sennecus.

The Incursor lifted his hand and inspected it. He flexed the red-stained armoured digits.

'Yes, lieutenant,' Sennecus replied. 'I ripped out the heart of a secessionist in our last engagement. The red mark is a trophy of our victory, brother-lieutenant.'

'Yes, I have heard of this "battle paint", brother.' Nemetus took a step closer and was about to deliver his chastisement when a voice cut across the muster hall.

'A fitting memorial to a traitor,' rasped Judiciar Admonius.

Armoured all in back, the Judiciar cut a sinister figure. At his waist hung a great hourglass, filled with dark sand: his tempormortis. Each grain came from the debris of Callosi station, a renegade installation atomised in the first engagement of Battle Group Faustus. Admonius' zealotry in that action had seen him recruited to the position of Judiciar, on the pathway to becoming a Chaplain.

The dedication that had drawn Admonius to the Reclusiam's ranks had increased with his acceptance, as if he were afraid that his status as novice would count against him. Nemetus knew better than to gainsay the Judiciar and instead raised a fist in salute.

'You are joining the boarding force, Brother-Judiciar?'

'Of course. It is my duty to prosecute the war against the traitors with every fervour. Did you think I would pass on this opportunity?'

Recognising the rhetoric in the question, Nemetus returned his attention to the warriors under his command.

'Brothers.' He took a breath, trying to ignore the nagging thoughts that came to him.

Self-aggrandisement.

Was he guilty of that crime?

'Brothers,' he began again, taking inspiration from his own mood. 'Some of you have raised your weapons beside me in battles before this day. Many of you have not, and indeed this is the first encounter with the foe since your preparatory missions. It matters not. We are all Adeptus Astartes. We are all sons of Lord Guilliman. We are all servants of the Emperor.'

He could not resist a glance towards Judiciar Admonius before he continued.

'It is not for ourselves that we fight, though we owe our brothers our commitment. We were created to spearhead a war far greater than any single warrior. Our foes seem without limit, but we will find it. We shall slay as many as needed, until the galaxy is secured once more for the dominion of humanity.'

He took another breath, settling into himself, finding direction from his own words.

'Remember that every blow you strike, every bolt you fire, is directed towards that single duty. Know also that at our backs stands the whole of the Imperium, its will bent to the reconquest of lost realms, the succour of enslaved worlds and the destruction of the dark enemy that has brought this wrath upon them. You are the implementation of that will. You are the Emperor's strength given form. Fight well and you shall not die, for your names shall live on ever after in glory!'

As his triumphant shout reverberated across the hall, Nemetus signalled the embarkation to begin. He felt Admonius beside him and turned his gaze on the Chaplain-in-Waiting.

'A fine speech,' said the Judiciar. 'Now let your deeds echo your words.'

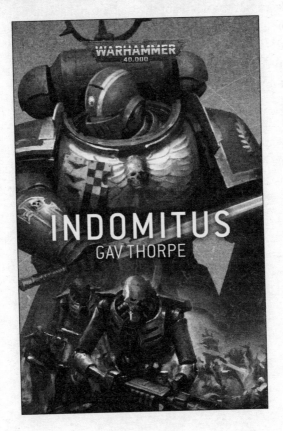

NEXUS

THOMAS PARROTT

CHAPTER 1

Sergeant Allectius sprinted through the trees towards the sounds of battle. Trunks blurred around him as he wove amongst the foliage with superhuman precision. A Space Marine standing by was a terrifying sight unto himself. It was seeing them move, however, that most often sparked 'transhuman dread' in mortals. It seemed impossible for something of such size and power to move so swiftly.

A pity, then, that the foe they faced seemed beyond fear.

The forest was filled with cacophony. The thunder of bolt weapons, the howl of chainswords and the odd sizzling whine of the xenos weaponry. The latter made his teeth ache every time he heard it, seeming to vibrate up and down his bones on some odd continuum. The former, however, was a comfort: his men were still alive, still fighting. For now.

Allectius saw the first knot of battle up ahead. Two of his brothers were duelling fiercely with a xenos horror. A skeletal torso surmounted a tripod of legs, skull face leering in its fixed grin. The forearms had been replaced; it had no more use for hands. Great blades ran down the sides instead, crackling with strange energies. Destroyers, they called them. Mindless abominations, whose only urge was to dismember and destroy. Even the necrons treated them like beasts, herding them into the foe. The sun-dappled beauty of their natural surroundings only made the stark horror stand out more.

The sergeant absorbed all of this in a beat of his dual hearts and angled towards the creature's back. Thoughtless the creature might be, but it did not diminish its deadliness. Even as he approached, one of its hyperphase swords slashed straight through the chainsword of the Astartes on its left. The blade carved on and through his torso, spraying blood across the greenery. His partner seized this opening and lunged forward, chainsword gouging a sparking hole in the monster's side.

The moment the Space Marine withdrew his weapon and stepped back from a counter swipe, the necron's wound began to close. Metal flowed together like liquid, sealing the opening as inner workings grew back together.

Allectius was there. It sensed his charge at the last second, turning its head. Too late. He aimed his plasma pistol, powered up to maximal mode, and fired. An incandescent blue-white beam of fury erupted from the sidearm. His war-plate's systems reported a heat spike just from holding the weapon. The coruscating blast struck the necron in the back and punched clean through the other side of it in an eruption of liquid metal and sizzling fragments. It continued on, scything through several trees before it had spent its ravening energy.

With a distorted, machine-like groan the xenos collapsed. Before it struck the ground, it was already shimmering with viridian light. The sergeant lunged forward, the chainsword in his other hand raised high. He brought it down with all of his might, but it passed through empty air with a *whoosh* and crunched into the ground. The severely damaged mechanoid had been teleported away. That was the way with the necrons. Only the utterly annihilated were not spirited off, presumably to be repaired and fight again.

Allectius' own men could not be saved so easily. He strode on to kneel beside the fallen Space Marine. The other man's in-built armour biodiagnosticator could be accessed via their squad noosphere. Brother Volusius was his name. The wound was serious, even for a Space Marine. A mortal man would have been struck dead instantly. Only the synthetic cells his genetically engineered Larraman's organ produced were keeping him from bleeding out, clotting faster than natural platelets ever could.

The sergeant activated the locator beacon built into the wounded warrior's plate, then stood. If the Apothecary reached him in time, he might be saved. If he did not, at least the fallen warrior's gene-seed could be salvaged.

'With me, Numonis,' he said.

'Until the end, brother-sergeant,' replied the other Assault Intercessor and fell in on his flank.

They hastened onward. It was not far before they erupted into a clearing that was the site of a raging battle. Two more of the Destroyers were locked in furious battle with the other four members of Allectius' squad. A third lumbered towards them, its blade-arms outstretched with mindless longing to rend. An insectile figure lurked in the wood line behind it. It had a solid body mounted on long legs, a strange mechanical proboscis waving in the air before it.

'Join the others, I will deal with the plasmacyte,' barked Allectius.

Numonis charged into the fray and the sergeant put his brothers from his mind. All were warriors of the Chapter, the finest mankind had to offer. He trusted them absolutely. For now, he had to focus all of his attention on his foe. His plasma pistol hummed in his left hand as his chainsword revved in the right. Distance-devouring strides carried him towards where the xenos machine lurked.

It skittered back into the shadows. Unlike their mindlessly destructive charges, the plasmacytes were often evasive. Their strength lay in the power they could infuse the Destroyers with, not in confrontation. Allectius' eyes narrowed, he had no intention of allowing it to escape so easily. He raised his plasma pistol and squeezed off a shot, counting on the power of the blast to carve through any intervening cover.

Instead, the weapon gave what could be described as a wheezing cough and powered down. The hydrogen flask was spent. A growing problem as the war for Cassothea dragged out. Allectius holstered the weapon and suppressed a growl of frustration. He would simply have to dismantle–

His thoughts were interrupted by the sudden lunge of the canoptek machine. It must have sensed weakness and activated new programming. There was no time to ponder. It was fast now that it was on the attack, lashing at him with the proboscis. The bladed tip was designed to punch through the living metal hide of a necron, and was more than capable of piercing his power armour if it connected right.

It struck at his face, aiming for his optic lenses. He ducked aside as fast as he could, diverting the strike to scrape a glancing hit along the side of his helmet instead. There was no chance to try to seize that machine tendril. It was striking now with its bladed legs. He caught the sweep of one on the edge of his chainsword, whirling teeth meeting the limb in a spray of sparks.

That monomolecular tip was stabbing at his face once more. Allectius was ready for it this time. With superhuman reflexes his hand flashed out and caught the proboscis, then with the other, he brought his chainsword around in a howling arc. It cleaved away in a flare of emerald fire. The machine staggered backwards, a strange mechanical warbling erupting from it.

The sergeant gave it no time to recover. He pushed forward as it retreated, hacking at the body now with the snarling blade. Each blow tore new rents in its mechanical hide, exposing the arcane workings of its innards. The Space Marine did his best to not commit any of that bizarreness to memory. He was no Techmarine, but even he understood that xenos machines were a corruption of technology. They were fit only to be destroyed.

He hacked away one of its legs and it toppled to the ground. The sergeant stomped on it with all his might, staving it in with a last eruption of viridian sparks that sizzled and flared into the underbrush. With a final strangled bleat it went still. He turned and charged back out into the clearing to find the combat there had entered its final moments.

Two of the Destroyers were gone, vanished back to whatever foul tomb birthed them. Haloed with green energies they shimmered into translucence and then were gone. It was not without cost: one of his brothers lay in the grass, dead, his head and arm hacked from his body by necron blades. The last of the twisted abominations found itself under the concentrated assault of all the remaining Space Marines at once.

They attacked in perfect concert, the product of years of elite training. Individually, they might not have been a match for the terrible mechanoid strength of a Destroyer. Yet their foe was a mindless butcher, while they were expert warriors. They carved it apart en masse. Then it was gone just as the others, little more than a green shimmer fading into nothing.

The sounds of battle died away, echoing off among the trees into silence. Allectius rested a hand against a nearby trunk for a moment. Adeptus Astartes did not tire as quickly and easily as mortals did, but the past months had been draining. Endless battle with little opportunity for recuperation. Skirmishes like this might have appeared to be victories to an outsider, but he knew better. The xenos defeated today would be repaired or replaced; their onslaught would not even slow. The Imperials had no such reinforcements on the way. The last allied warship to arrive in-system had been so badly damaged from some unknown catastrophe it had crashed behind enemy lines.

The sergeant let his arm fall back to his side. It would not do to let the men see any weakness on his part. He activated the vox-link to central command.

'Redoubt Primus, this is Squad Allectius. Our patrol encountered resistance in the Sanral Wood. Destroyers accompanied by plasmacyte. They've been neutralised. One of our brothers has fallen and one needs medicae retrieval.'

'*Acknowledged, Squad Allectius.*' Allectius recognised the voice as Dacien, one of the serfs who worked the comms. There was a curious reticence in his voice. '*Return to base immediately.*'

Allectius frowned. 'Our strength is not depleted, Redoubt Primus. We can continue the patrol.'

There was an extended pause. '*Negative, Squad Allectius. Come back with all speed.*' There was a note of real distress in that voice.

The sergeant narrowed his eyes. It was possible the serf was exceeding his authority in this matter. It was not an argument to have on the vox, however. 'Acknowledged. Squad Allectius on the move. We will bring our casualties with us.' He gave a single sigh and switched his vox-channel back to the squad network. 'We are to return to the redoubt, brothers. Collect Volusius and Landrian. We shall see them home ourselves.'

Allectius scanned the treeline one last time to make sure there were no further enemies lurking about. In the back of his mind, however, that hitch in the serf's voice lingered. Misguided the mortal might be, but something had shaken him. With any luck, he would have answers soon.

Squad Allectius walked amongst the skeletons of burned out buildings. Autocarriage wrecks were piled up in the streets, many showing the tell-tale 'peeling' of necron gauss weaponry. A stillness pervaded the devastation. It made the heavy tread of the Space Marines seem even louder than normal, echoing from broken glass and crumpled metal. The sound came back strange, set him on edge. He was relieved when he saw the great slab of rockcrete up ahead.

Redoubt Primus was what remained of Cassothea's capital city. Allectius had been told the name once. Macuth. It did not matter now. It was ruins. They had tried to defend it against the necron onslaught during the first month, but it had been a lost cause from the beginning. The defence efforts contracted with each assault, a shrinking ring that left a growing number of civilians on the outside.

Some rioted. The smart ones fled into the countryside. It was a poor hope, but still a more likely chance out in the wilderness. There, at least, they might go unnoticed by the xenos death-machines that stalked the landscape. Here they were penned in and slaughtered. The enemy had no remorse. It felt no mercy. They had set out to cleanse this world for their obscure purposes, and if any moral compunctions entered their equations then Allectius had not been able to discern them.

All were long gone now. Only the bodies remained. Those who had fallen in the streets had long since mummified. Bodies left in the shade had decayed down to dry bones. Those caught by the most powerful weapons had disintegrated completely. Their dust layered the interiors of the buildings and blew in clouds through the streets. All of them, those the Ultramarines had not been able to protect. Adeptus Astartes were hardened, their minds reinforced by years of hypno-conditioning and training. For all that, it ate at Allectius. A helplessness that he could only express through fury.

The citizenry were evacuating now, transports taking them and any resources they could carry away as fast as possible. That was the purpose of the patrol today, and others like it. Try to find what survivors and abandoned materiel they could and get them off-world. Perhaps if they had known the odds from the beginning, more might have been saved. Perhaps not. The crusade's leadership had said this world must be saved, and so they had tried. Failure was not something Space Marines were accustomed to.

They were approaching the walls of the fortress now. Allectius had never been to Macragge, the home world of the Ultramarines – awoken from stasis by Archmagos Cawl with the Imperium torn asunder, he had been on crusade ever since. He had seen pict-captures, however. Even the fortifications there were beautiful, built with strength and aesthetics both. There was nothing pleasing about the sight of Redoubt Primus. It was squat and undecorated. Only thick walls could withstand the molecular stripping of gauss weapons.

Tarantula sentry guns bristled from emplacements. They came in a variety of shapes: assault cannons and heavy bolters for the enemy infantry, lascannons and multi-meltas for the armour. There were even missile launchers to help defend against aerial attack. It all looked quite formidable. Unfortunately, looks could deceive. Ammo supplies were running low. Most of these guns would fall silent within minutes of an attack beginning.

The sergeant paused as the auspexes scanned him and his men. He pulled his helmet off with a hiss of depressurisation, the brush of a cool breeze on his sweaty face welcome. Once their identities were confirmed, the great adamantine gates began to slide open. More than a dozen serfs rushed out to help get the wounded inside, overseen by Apothecary Calvus. The white-armoured brother handled the medicae needs of the Space Marines, and when necessary harvested the gene-seed from the bodies of the fallen. Only by carefully preserving the Chapter's due in this way could future initiates be raised to the transhuman level of the Space Marines.

'It is good to see you again, Brother Allectius,' said Calvus.

'The same to you, Brother-Apothecary,' the sergeant replied. They clasped gauntlets briefly. 'Do you know why we were recalled?'

'I do.' It was not the Apothecary's way to mince words. 'Yet I have work to attend to seeing to your casualties. Find Chaplain Sisenna. He will explain.'

Allectius nodded. 'I will leave them in your capable hands and seek him out.' He turned to the rest of his squad. 'Take the time to resupply. We may be fighting again at any moment.'

Each pressed a fist to their chests in response and the sergeant turned away to stride into the dark of the base. The structure had, by necessity, been sized to accommodate the build of a Space Marine, but the rush of construction left it a tight fit nevertheless. Glow-globes fixed on the ceiling brushed his head as he passed under them, nearly forcing him to duck aside. Most were kept dim; power supplies were just as rationed as everything else these days.

Allectius passed the refectory on his right. It was quiet save the murmur of conversation and the clink of dinnerware. The briny scent of hard rations was on the air – fresh food had become an unthinkable luxury as the xenos noose tightened. He could spot his brothers easily enough, of course; their stature made them stand out if nothing else would. The rest of those gathered were a mix of serfs and locals, but it was becoming hard to tell them apart. Heraldry was greying into unrecognisability by weathering and grime.

The sergeant could not help but notice the reaction his presence drew. A hush of conversation, stares. It added to his disquiet and he hurried on. The sounds and smells faded as he continued, replaced by the growing spice-and-lemon scent of incense.

As he drew closer to the chapel, the hallway began to be lined by posts. Each held a token of some sort. Here, the shattered fragments of a plasma gun. There, a purity seal that had nearly burned away. It had begun as a stop gap, temporary honours for fallen brothers. Whole suits of armour then. Now all that remained was what could not be salvaged and repurposed.

There had been ninety-three warriors in the company when they had arrived at Cassothea. There had been talk of picking up reinforcements before proceeding to the next campaign. That had been fifty-six dead brothers ago. Their totems had overrun the chapel and spilled out into the passageways. There was nothing faceless about their memories. He had known these men for years, fought alongside them. Now they were gone.

Allectius could hear the words now, in Sisenna's powerful rumble.

Lord Guilliman, Avenging Son,
Guide us in battle.
Steel us against the trickery of the xenos.
Make of us scourges of the Emperor's foes.
Aid us, O gene-father and primarch,
As we lay our righteous fury upon the alien.
For our enemies are many,
And seek the ruin of all mankind.

The sergeant stepped into the chapel. Six Ultramarines knelt before the Chaplain, their heads bowed. Allectius recognised the men of Squad Two, led by Sergeant Proclus. Another patrol, preparing to continue the search. Sisenna stood before them, a compelling sight in his black armour and skull-mask. His staff of office, the crozius arcanum, was held in front of him as he intoned the rite. He met Allectius' gaze and gave him a slight nod of recognition. The sergeant returned the gesture and stood to the back to wait.

Each member of Squad Two stepped forward to be blessed, touched on each pauldron by the aquila of the crozius. Then they stepped past the Chaplain to a particular totem. A helmet hung there, surmounted by a crest of once-brilliant red and white. Now it was faded and dingy. The headgear itself would have been salvageable. It had been left in place nonetheless, the only small honour the company could still offer its fallen commander.

Each saluted in turn to the memory of the company commander, and turned to depart. Proclus himself was the last to step forward and accept his blessings. The other sergeant turned when he was done and offered Allectius a sad smile. He paused only to briefly rest a gauntlet on Allectius' shoulder. He departed with his squad. The Squad Four sergeant watched him go uneasily.

'Brother Allectius, how are you?' The Chaplain's voice brought his head around. Sisenna removed his skull-helm and set it aside. The face revealed was broad and tawny, broken by lighter streaks of a number of scars. One marked through his eye – that orb had been replaced by the cold red light of a bionic.

'Ill at ease, Brother-Chaplain, if I am to be honest with you,' replied the sergeant.

Sisenna stepped over to light new incense. The flicker of flame cast his face into a sharp divide of light and shadow. 'What troubles you?'

Allectius laughed without humour at that. 'What does not? Our enemy closes in. I am recalled from duty early, my mission incomplete. I am the subject of whispers and stares. Even the Apothecary tells me merely to seek you out.'

The Chaplain turned to face him once more and waited patiently.

Allectius flexed his hands, then the words tore out of him. 'Is my honour called into question?'

'Ah, there it is,' said Sisenna quietly. 'No.' He gestured away. 'We must always strive to do better than the day before. Our calling is the highest. If we are not improving, we are dying. All of that said, you are not here to be reproached.'

The sergeant took a calming breath. 'Then what is the matter? If we were being reassigned, word would come from the lieutenant.'

'That strikes to the very heart of the matter,' said the Chaplain. He paused, an uncharacteristic hesitation, before continuing, 'Falerius is dead.'

'No,' breathed Allectius. Another wound on his soul, another loss to be borne. Lieutenant Falerius had been forced to take command when the senior lieutenant died in the opening days of the conflict. He had held the company together through the tough fighting of the past months. 'How?'

'Squad Three was pinned down by hostiles in the city ruins. Falerius led the Bladeguard into battle to rescue them. They could get the brothers out, but the enemy had posted Death-marks in the surrounding buildings.' Deathmarks were the deadly snipers of the necron forces. The rest the sergeant could imagine.

Allectius closed his eyes. 'An honourable death,' was all he could manage.

Sisenna nodded. 'It also leads to your involvement. With all the officer cadre dead, command would usually fall to the senior sergeant.'

'As the Codex Astartes dictates,' agreed Allectius. 'I am fully prepared to accept Sergeant Fulgentius' command.'

The Chaplain shook his head now. 'That is not to be. Fal-erius left specific instructions on what should happen in the case of his death.' He locked eyes with Allectius. 'He named you, Allectius. You are hereby promoted to lieuten-ant, pending the confirmation of the Chapter Master to make it official, of course.'

Allectius could only stare at him for a moment. Finally, he managed, 'What?'

'You are in command of the company now, lieutenant.' Sisenna stepped forward and rested a hand on his shoul-der. 'I believe you will rise to this challenge. The sergeants have agreed to abide by the decision. We are behind you, one and all.'

The newly minted lieutenant searched for words. 'I–'

Before he could find them, something fundamental in the cosmos shifted. An oppressive weight fell upon the very essence of the world. Colours faded and lights dimmed. It hit Allectius like suffocation, as if the air was too still to be able to breathe. He had to force it into his lungs, and could feel his hearts pound. There was no question it went beyond him – he could see that Chaplain Sisenna had staggered a step, his face twisted in his surprise.

That was when his vox-rig crackled. *'Forgive me, but we need the lieutenant in the command centre right now.'* The communication serf sounded strained, in real pain. *'We're getting distress calls from the evacuation ships. Something has gone wrong.'*

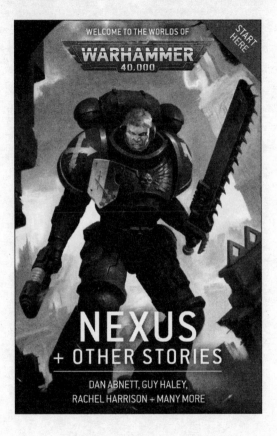

THE DEVASTATION
OF BAAL

GUY HALEY

CHAPTER ONE

THE RED MIST

Already the morning gongs were ringing when Uigui the water seller roused himself for another day of thankless toil.

Uigui rose fully clothed, and went to empty his bladder into the home-made purification unit in the corner. Every drop of water was precious on Baal Secundus, whatever the source.

His single-roomed home held three cots, a table, the recyc unit and precious little else. Old transit pallets heaped with threadbare blankets against the cold of desert night were their beds. On the way to the recyc unit, Uigui passed his great burden, his idiot son. The boy had gone away to the Chapter trials full of hope, and come back minus his wits.

'Get up! Up! Up, you little fool!' Uigui kicked at his son's booted feet. The boy thrashed awake and threw up his hands in alarm. A frightened face peeped out between filthy fingers.

'Get up!' growled Uigui. 'Dawn's coming – can't you hear the Angel's gongs?' He looked out of a window of low-grade alabaster set into the wall of unpainted adobe. Daybreak should have shone pink through the stone. Instead a red darkness lingered outside.

Most mornings were cold but beautiful, the sky flawlessly smooth and tinted a deep rose by the light of the Red Scar. Sometimes, the colours were enough to stop Uigui and make him forget how much he hated his life. 'Not that you can tell,' grunted Uigui. 'Red mist. A thick one too.'

'D-d-d-d-do we-e-e have to, Da?' said the boy.

Uigui looked at the boy with clear hatred as he urinated into the recyc funnel. 'Y-y-yes!' he spat back, mocking the boy's stutter. 'Now, up! I need help to fill the flasks, age be cursed, or I'd turn you over to the Emperor's mercy and be rid of you!'

Uigui adjusted his filthy clothes and stamped, bow backed and swaying, to the door of gappy wood that separated the single room of his home from the goods yard outside. He clutched at his lower back as he reached for the door handle and rubbed fruitlessly at the pain in his bones, his mood souring further.

'Be kinder to the boy. He is my daughter's son,' croaked the aged voice of the room's final occupant. The coverings on the third bed shifted, the lump beneath them growing thin arms and knotted hands as a woman even more wasted and hunched than Uigui emerged. 'You owe him some love for her memory, if you can't summon some for the boy himself.'

The old woman coughed hard. Phlegm rattled around her throat. Uigui looked at her in disgust. Her face was as deeply lined as the pit of a fruit, as if time had rotted away the pleasant outer flesh, leaving the bitter, craggy interior of her soul exposed for all to see.

'Where's your daughter now, you old witch?' he said. 'Dead. Dead and gone, leaving me with a fool and a crone for company.'

'You are cruel,' said the old woman. Clustered carcinomas blighted her face. She had only a few more months of life in her, but her eyes were bright and shrewd. Uigui hated her eyes most of all. 'The Emperor will punish you.'

Uigui snarled. 'We'll all starve long before the Emperor notices if you and your precious grandson don't rouse yourselves. We must be at the gates before they open for the day.'

The woman shrank back into her blankets. 'The Red Mist is here. You will have no customers.'

Uigui rested his hand on the piece of scrap he had fashioned into the door handle. It was worn almost featureless. He had unearthed the metal in his youth from one of the moon's ruined cities. An unidentifiable artefact of the system's lost paradisal past, it could once have been a piece of art, it could have been a component from a wondrous machine. It could have been anything. Now it was old, ugly and broken, suitable only for the coarsest work. Just like Uigui.

'Then we will starve. Get up. We go to work.' He flipped the door open, letting it bang into the wall to show his anger.

The Red Mist was the worst he'd ever seen: a choking, thick vapour laden with sand particles. Only on a low gravity lunar body like Baal Secundus was such a phenomenon possible, though Uigui didn't know that. His worldview was necessarily limited. What he saw was a day's business ruined. Red Mist was iron sharp in smell and texture, a soupy brume that lacerated the nostrils. He coughed and pulled up his scarf to cover his mouth and nose. He had no clip to hold it in place, so he pressed it to the contours of his face with his left hand.

Though his home was modest, his stockyard contained a

fortune. Four huge terracotta urns, taller than men and too wide for the embrace of two people to meet around, lined the wall. With such wealth to protect, the courtyard was better built than the house. The walls were of stone, not mud brick, and high, the tops studded with rusty spikes and broken glass. The gate was deliberately small, triple-barred, plated in scavenged metal, upon whose pocked surfaces the marks of the ancients were still visible, when the light was right.

There was no sun. The early day was tainted a bloody murk. The urns were looming shapes, the wall invisible. The yard was little over twenty feet side to side, but the Red Mist was so dense that day Uigui could not see across.

He paused. At the very least the fog would be full of toxins given off by Baal Secundus' poisoned seas. If the sands in the mist had been picked up over one of the old cities, the rad levels would be high. Uigui supposed he should fetch his rad-ticker from inside. Frankly, he could not motivate himself to retrieve it. He was old. A dose of radiation from the badlands could not shorten his life by much, and if it did, what of it? He was tired of life. It was hard and unforgiving.

Sometimes he thought of ending it all, the misery, the graft, the wearing company of his son and mother-in-law. He had no illusions death would bring a happy afterlife in the Emperor's care; all he wanted was peace. He could not bring himself to do it. The mindless will of genes forced him to continue living, which he did begrudgingly.

Blinking gritty moisture from his eyes, he headed for the lean-to where he kept his cart. A pair of tall wheels bracketed two cargo beds, one above the other. Three dozen clay flasks were on each level. He fetched the first and took it to the tap attached to the nearest urn. To fill it he had to let his scarf drop. The dust in the mist tickled his nose and he swore.

Rusty water ran into the bottle, making him want to piss again. His bladder was another thing that was failing him.

'Boy! Boy! Get out here and help me!'

The door creaked. Out came the old woman instead, her face veiled in the ridiculous manner of her desert tribe. Uigui should never have married out of town.

'Where's that damn boy?' growled Uigui.

'Let him breakfast, you old miser, he'll be out in a moment.'

'He's a waste of food and water,' said Uigui. He shut off the tap, pressed the cap closed on the bottle and fetched another flask.

'It's not his fault,' said the old woman.

'I think we all know that it's the Angel's fault,' said Uigui quietly.

'Hsst!' she said. 'That is heresy. Would you leave him without a father as well as his mind?'

'He went to their trials a strong youth, and was returned to me a fool. Who else should I blame?'

'Fate,' she said. 'He was not meant to join them, and he is getting better.'

'He is not,' said Uigui sourly. He set the full flask into his cart, and fetched a third.

The crone shuffled across the courtyard to the cart, her long skirts disturbing the moist sand of the ground. There she stopped, but she did not help, only watched him, a judgemental phantom in the fog. Uigui gave her a filthy look.

In her gnarled hands a small auto-tarot deck made its tooth-grinding clicks. She pushed the button at the side. The tiles behind its scratched viewing pane clattered into place. She studied the little pictures on them a moment, then pressed the button again. Then again. Uigui fought the urge to strike her, to knock the tarot from her hand and cast her out. The tarot was the instrument of the Emperor. Even he balked at such blasphemy.

'Help me, then,' he said. He squinted at the sky. 'The sun is rising.' The fog remained as thick as ever, but the light behind it was getting stronger. 'We are late.'

The old woman hooked her tarot deck to her rope belt, took a flask up and went to the second urn.

'Today is a day of great portents,' she said.

'You say that every day,' said Uigui.

The woman shrugged. 'Today it is true.'

'Nonsense,' he said, but he was wary of what she said. She had a knack for reading the tarot. He half believed she was a witch. In truth, he was frightened of her. He slammed the latest filled flask into the cart hard, making the others rattle. 'Where is that boy?'

The boy pushed the cart. At least he was good for that. Uigui and the old woman walked behind. The flasks knocked and clinked in their trays, warning others they were coming. It was a good advertisement, but under the cover of the fog the noise made Uigui nervous. For all that Angel's Fall was under the direct administration of the Blood Angels, there was always the possibility of robbery on a day of mist.

They met no misfortune as they walked the street from Waterer's Row towards the Sanguinian Way, the small city's main street. There were precious few people about. Those figures that appeared suddenly out of the murk were swaddled head to foot, and just as quickly disappeared.

'Quicker, boy,' grumbled Uigui. 'We want a good spot. I want to get there before they are all gone.'

They turned onto the Sanguinian Way. At its far end was the Place of Choosing, where the giant statue of the Great Angel spread his arms and wings to face the eastern sky. Immense though Sanguinius' effigy was, the fog obscured it totally. With the majestic statue hidden, the cramped, low buildings that made up Angel's Fall seemed ruder than ever. It did not look like a holy city. The fog forced attention onto its inadequacies. Even the Sanguinian Way was meanly proportioned, and crooked. Without Sanguinius, Angel's Fall could have been any town on any backward, arid world in the galaxy.

Gongs boomed from unseen towers, signifying the start of the Peaceday markets. Only a handful of stalls had been set up at the roadside, and foot traffic on the way was low. Uigui reckoned visitors to Angel's Fall would be fewer than usual, though there were always some. The Red Mist discouraged travel. Not only was it toxic, but Baal's violent wildlife hunted under its cover. He cursed his luck. Water was expensive to both the buyer and the seller. The price he'd get for his stock barely covered the cost, and he owed a lot of money to Anton the reguliser. Anton took prompt payment of debts very seriously. Uigui rubbed at the stump of his left little finger, a reminder of the last time he'd been late with a payment. Anton had been nothing but apologetic; he had said he had no choice.

Uigui thought they would have to stay out late, selling to people exiting the city to travel in the cool of the night. *Assuming the mist lifts today at all*, he fretted. Such a fog was rare. Baal Secundus' principal weathers were wind and dust storms, but there was not a breath of a breeze today.

'This weather is unnatural,' he said.

'A day of portents,' said his mother-in-law in satisfaction.

'Shut up,' he said. 'It's just a day. Boy. Here.' Uigui pointed out a patch of ground in the lee of the Temple of the Emperor. The temple occupied a whole block by itself, and another of

Angel's Fall's major streets intersected the Sanguinian Way there.

'This will do.' The gongs continued to ring. 'Why all this racket?' Uigui said.

'Happenings. Baalfora has much in store for us today,' said the old woman, using the local name for Baal Secundus. She settled herself down. Her joints grumbled, and she grumbled back at them, forcing her old legs to cross. Upon skirts held taut between her knees she set her tarot deck and began repetitively clicking at the workings. Uigui bared his teeth at her. He took out his irritation on the boy.

'Come on, boy, set out the table! Where are the cups? By the Emperor, we'd all die if you were in charge here!'

'S-s-s-orry, father,' said the boy.

'Don't call me that,' he said. 'My son is dead. Stolen by angels. There is no one to inherit my business once I am gone. Do not presume your place.'

The boy bowed his head to hide his tears, showing the ugly scar running across the top of his head. Uigui hated the sight of that most of all. He was sure had his boy not fallen he would be up there on Baal as a warrior of the Emperor. He stared at it as the boy set up the little table that folded out from the side of the cart and put out a set of small bronze cups. Something like grief hurt him. He responded with anger.

'Quicker!' he snapped.

The gongs were still booming long after they should have stopped. He squinted into the dim morning. There was another sound, a distant rumbling, under the clamour of the gongs.

'What is that?' he whispered.

'V-v-void ships?' ventured the boy.

'Silence!' snapped Uigui. But even as his anger flew out of his mouth, he thought the boy might be right. Angel's Fall was no stranger to the ships of the Angels. There were off-worlders too, who came to pay their respects to the place where Sanguinius, purest of the Emperor's progeny, was discovered. But rarely did they arrive in such numbers that the sound of their descent was so constant.

Uigui heard the crunch of heavy feet on sand coming down the way. He swore at himself. Angels. They would have no use for his water.

'Bow! Bow!' he hissed. He dropped his head, and forced his idiot son to kneel.

A huge armoured figure emerged from the murk. Armour black, his helm cast in the shape of a skull. A Space Marine priest, death incarnate. Uigui trembled. He dropped to his knees in fright, waiting for the figure to pass by.

He did not. The footsteps stopped by the little cart. Uigui felt the Angel's regard upon him. His bladder twinged yet again.

'Be at peace, blessed son of Baal Secundus,' said the warrior. His voice was inhumanly deep and thickly accented.

Uigui looked up. The grimacing skull glared down at him. Breathing hoses were clamped between its stylised teeth, and eye-lenses of glowing green set below the angry brow. The armour hissed and whined in response to microshifts in the Space Marine's posture, making Uigui more afraid.

The warrior looked down both streets of the crossroads.

'The great square. Where is it?'

Though made hollow and booming by its projection machinery, the warrior's voice was kindly. Still Uigui could not see past the terrible visage glowering at him. He stared dumbly back.

'Waterseller, I mean you no harm,' said the Angel. 'I come to pay my respects to my lord. Where is his statue?'

Uigui trembled and flung up his arm. He intended to say 'That way, my lord!' A strangled mewl came out of his mouth instead.

'My thanks, and my blessings,' said the Chaplain. 'The Emperor keep you.'

He glanced up at the great temple, then strode away.

'W-w-why does he not know?' said the boy stupidly.

'I do not know,' said Uigui. Still upon his knees he gazed fearfully at the departing giant.

'M-m-m-more!' said the boy, and shrank back behind the cart.

Uigui followed his son's wavering finger. More Space Marines, dozens of them. Uigui had never seen so many at one time and his body shook in terror. They walked past, armour dull in the foggy daylight. Uigui could see clearly enough to know they were not Blood Angels. Their armour was adorned in a similar manner to that of the masters of Baal. The heavy plates were beautifully formed, covered in scrollwork and delicate embellishments, and decked with bloodstone drips cased in gold, but the red of their armour was an unfamiliar hue, their helms and trim were white, and their markings were strange.

Uigui watched, amazed, as the column of warriors moved by in solemn silence, voiceless but for the growls and hum of their armour. It was not unusual to see other angels claiming descent from the Great Angel in Angel's Fall, but only in ones or twos. When a second group in yet different colours marched by, these armoured half in black and half in bloody red, Uigui's mouth fell open. The gongs boomed. Outside the wall, the roaring of braking jets grew louder.

'Th-th-there's hundreds of them!' stuttered the boy.

For a moment, Uigui forgot his anger, and put his arm around his broken son.

'W-w-w-why so many?' the boy said.

'They come to pay respect to their father. They come to pray,' said Uigui. 'It is a marvel.'

The old woman chuckled, a low growling sound like a felid about to bite. The tarot tiles rattled.

'What is it?' Uigui said.

The old woman's smile was evident in her voice. 'The burning tower, the bloody angel, the falling star, the foundered void ship – these are fell signs.'

Uigui looked sharply back at her. 'What do you mean?'

The old woman regarded him through the cloth of her veil. 'They are not coming here to worship, you foolish man,' she said. 'They have come here to die.'

YOUR
NEXT READ

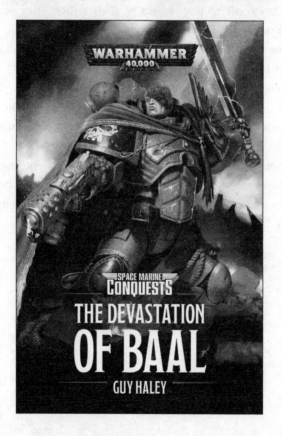

THE DEVASTATION OF BAAL
by Guy Haley

Baal is besieged! The alien horror of Hive Fleet Leviathan has reached the Blood Angels home world, and their entire existence is under threat. As the sons of Sanguinius gather, the battle for the fate of their bloodline begins…

XENOS

DAN ABNETT

ONE

Hunting the recidivist Murdin Eyclone, I came to Hubris in the Dormant of 240.M41, as the Imperial sidereal calendar has it.

Dormant lasted eleven months of Hubris's twenty-nine month lunar year, and the only signs of life were the custodians with their lighted poles and heat-gowns, patrolling the precincts of the hibernation tombs.

Within those sulking basalt and ceramite vaults, the grandees of Hubris slept, dreaming in crypts of aching ice, awaiting Thaw, the middle season between Dormant and Vital.

Even the air was frigid. Frost encrusted the tombs, and a thick cake of ice covered the featureless land. Above, star patterns twinkled in the curious, permanent night. One of them was Hubris's sun, so far away now. Come Thaw, Hubris would spin into the warm embrace of its star again.

Then it would become a blazing globe. Now it was just a fuzz of light.

As my gun-cutter set down on the landing cross at Tomb Point, I had pulled on an internally heated bodyskin and swathes of sturdy, insulated foul weather gear, but still the perilous cold cut through me now. My eyes watered, and the tears froze on my lashes and cheeks. I remembered the details of the cultural brief my savant had prepared, and quickly lowered my frost visor, trembling as warm air began to circulate under the plastic mask.

Custodians, alerted to my arrival by astropathic hails, stood waiting for me at the base of the landing cross. Their lighted poles dipped in obeisance in the frozen night and the air steamed with the heat that bled from their cloaks. I nodded to them, showing their leader my badge of office. An ice-car awaited: a rust-coloured arrowhead twenty metres long, mounted on ski-blade runners and spiked tracks.

It carried me away from the landing cross and I left the winking signal lights and the serrated dagger-shape of my gun-cutter behind in the perpetual winter night.

The spiked tracks kicked up blizzards of rime behind us. Ahead, despite the lamps, the landscape was black and impenetrable. I rode with Lores Vibben and three custodians in a cabin lit only by the amber glow of the craft's control panel. Heating vents recessed in the leather seats breathed out warm, stale air.

A custodian handed back a data-slate to Vibben. She looked at it cursorily and passed it on to me. I realised my frost visor was still down. I raised it and began to search my pockets for my eye glasses.

With a smile, Vibben produced them from within her own swaddled, insulated garb. I nodded thanks, put them on my nose and began to read.

I was just calling up the last plates of text when the ice-car halted.

'Processional Two-Twelve,' announced one of the custodians.

We dismounted, sliding our visors down into place.

Jewels of frost-flakes fluttered in the blackness about us, sparkling as they crossed through the ice-car's lamp beams. I've heard of bitter cold. Emperor grace me I never feel it again. Biting, crippling, actually bitter to taste on the tongue. Every joint in my frame protested and creaked.

My hands and my mind were numb.

That was not good.

Processional Two-Twelve was a hibernation tomb at the west end of the great Imperial Avenue. It housed twelve thousand, one hundred and forty-two members of the Hubris ruling elite.

We approached the great monument, crunching up the black, frost-coated steps.

I halted. 'Where are the tomb's custodians?'

'Making their rounds,' I was told.

I glanced at Vibben and shook my head. She slid her hand into her fur-edged robes.

'Knowing we approach?' I urged, addressing the custodian again. 'Knowing we expect to meet them?'

'I will check,' said the custodian, the one who had circulated the slate. He pushed on up the steps, the phosphor light on his pole bobbing.

The other two seemed ill at ease.

I beckoned to Vibben, so she would follow me up after the leader.

We found him on a lower terrace, gazing at the strewn bodies of four custodians, their light poles fizzling out around them.

'H-how?' he stammered.

'Stay back,' Vibben told him and drew her weapon. Its tiny amber Armed rune glowed in the darkness.

I took out my blade, igniting it. It hummed.

The south entry of the tombs was open. Shafts of golden light shone out. All my fears were rapidly being confirmed.

We entered, Vibben sweeping the place from side to side with her handgun. The hall was narrow and high, lit by chemical glow-globes. Intruding frost was beginning to mark the polished basalt walls.

A few metres inside, another custodian lay dead in a stiffening mirror of blood. We stepped over him. To each side, hallways opened up, admitting us to the hibernation stacks. In every direction, rows and rows of ice-berths ranged down the smoothed basalt chambers.

It was like walking into the Imperium's grandest morgue.

Vibben swept soundlessly to the right and I went left.

I admit I was excited by now, eager to close and conclude a business that had lasted six years. Eyclone had evaded me for six whole years! I studied his methods every day and dreamed of him every night.

Now I could smell him.

I raised my visor.

Water was pattering from the roof. Thaw water. It was growing warmer in here. In their ice-berths, some of the dim figures were stirring.

Too early! Far too early!

Eyclone's first man came at me from the west as I crossed a trunk-junction corridor. I spun, the power sword in my hand, and cut through his neck before his ice-axe could land.

The second came from the south, the third from the east. And then more. More.

A blur.

As I fought, I heard furious shooting from the vaults away to my right. Vibben was in trouble.

I could hear her over the vox-link in our hoods: 'Eisenhorn! Eisenhorn!'

I wheeled and cut. My opponents were all dressed in heatgowns, and carried ice-tools that made proficient weapons. Their eyes were dark and unforthcoming. Though they were fast, there was something in them that suggested they were doing this mindlessly, by order.

The power sword, an antique and graceful weapon, blessed by the Provost of Inx himself, spun in my hand. With five abrupt moves I made corpses out of them and left their blood vapour drifting in the air.

'Eisenhorn!'

I turned and ran. I splashed heavily down a corridor sluiced with melt water. More shots from ahead. A sucking cry.

I found Vibben face down across a freezer tube, frozen blood gluing her to the sub-zero plastic. Eight of Eyclone's servants lay sprawled around her. Her weapon lay just out of reach of her clawing hand, the spent cell ejected from the grip.

I am forty-two standard years old, in my prime by Imperial standards, young by those of the Inquisition. All my life, I have had a reputation for being cold, unfeeling. Some have called me heartless, ruthless, even cruel. I am not. I am not beyond emotional response or compassion. But I possess – and my masters count this as perhaps my paramount virtue – a singular force of will. Throughout my career it has served me well to draw on this facility and steel myself, unflinching, at all that this wretched galaxy can throw at me. To feel pain or fear or grief is to allow myself a luxury I cannot afford.

Lores Vibben had served with me for five and a half years. In that period she had saved my life twice. She saw herself as my aide and my bodyguard, yet in truth she was more a companion and a fellow warrior. When I recruited her from the clan-slums of Tornish, it was for her combat skills and brutal vigour. But I came to value her just as much for her sharp mind, soft wit and clear head.

I stared down at her body for a moment. I believe I may have uttered her name.

I extinguished my power sword and, sliding it into its scabbard, moved back into the shadows on the far side of the hibernation gallery. I could hear nothing except the increasingly persistent thaw-drip. Freeing my sidearm from its leather rig under my left armpit, I checked its load and opened a vox link. Eyclone was undoubtedly monitoring all traffic in and out of Processional Two-Twelve, so I used Glossia, an informal verbal cipher known only to myself and my immediate colleagues. Most inquisitors develop their own private languages for confidential communication, some more sophisticated than others. Glossia, the basics of which I had designed ten years before, was reasonably complex and had evolved, organically, with use.

'Thorn wishes aegis, rapturous beasts below.'

'Aegis, arising, the colours of space,' Betancore responded immediately and correctly.

'Rose thorn, abundant, by flame light crescent.'

A pause. 'By flame light crescent? Confirm.'

'Confirm.'

'Razor delphus pathway! Pattern ivory!'

'Pattern denied. Pattern crucible.'

'Aegis, arising.'

The link broke. He was on his way. He had taken the news of Vibben's death as hard as I expected. I trusted that would not affect his performance. Midas Betancore was a hot-blooded, impetuous man, which was partly why I liked him. And used him.

I moved out of the shadows again, my sidearm raised. A Scipio-pattern naval pistol, finished in dull chrome with inlaid ivory grips, it felt reassuringly heavy in my gloved hand. Ten rounds, every one a fat, blunt man-stopper, were spring-loaded into the slide inside the grip. I had four more armed slides just like it in my hip pocket.

I forget where I acquired the Scipio. It had been mine for a few years. One night, three years before, Vibben had prised off the ceramite grip plates with their touch-worn, machined-stamped engravings of the Imperial aquila and the Navy motto, and replaced them with ivory grips she had etched herself. A common practice on Tornish, she informed me, handing the weapon back the next day. The new grips were like crude scrimshaw, showing on each side a poorly executed human skull through which a thorny rose entwined, emerging through an eye socket, shedding cartoon droplets of blood. She'd inlaid carmine gems into the droplets to emphasise their nature. Below the skull, my name was scratched in a clumsy scroll.

I had laughed. There had been times when I'd almost been too embarrassed to draw the gang-marked weapon in a fight.

Now, now she was dead, I realise what an honour had been paid to me through that devoted work.

I made a promise to myself: I would kill Eyclone with this gun.

As a devoted member of his high majesty the God-Emperor's Inquisition, I find my philosophy bends towards that of the

Amalathians. To the outside galaxy, members of our orders appear much alike: an inquisitor is an inquisitor, a being of fear and persecution. It surprises many that internally, we are riven with clashing ideologies.

I know it surprised Vibben. I spent one long afternoon trying to explain the differences. I failed.

To express it in simple terms, some inquisitors are puritans and some are radicals. Puritans believe in and enforce the traditional station of the Inquisition, working to purge our galactic community of any criminal or malevolent element: the triumvirate of evil – alien, mutant and daemon. Anything that clashes with the pure rule of mankind, the preachings of the Ministorum and the letter of Imperial Law is subject to a puritan inquisitor's attention. Hard-line, traditional, merciless… that is the puritan way.

Radicals believe that any methods are allowable if they accomplish the Inquisitorial task. Some, as I understand it, actually embrace and use forbidden resources, such as the Warp itself, as weapons against the enemies of mankind.

I have heard the arguments often enough. They appal me. Radical belief is heretical.

I am a puritan by calling and an Amalathian by choice. The ferociously strict ways of the monodominant philosophy oft-times entices me, but there is precious little subtlety in their ways and thus it is not for me.

Amalathians take our name from the conclave at Mount Amalath. Our endeavour is to maintain the status quo of the Imperium, and we work to identify and destroy any persons or agencies that might destabilise the power of the Imperium from without or within. We believe in strength through unity. Change is the greatest enemy. We believe the God-Emperor has a divine plan, and we work to sustain the Imperium in stability until that plan is made known. We deplore factions and in-fighting... Indeed, it is sometimes a painful irony that our beliefs mark us as a faction within the political helix of the Inquisition.

We are the steadfast spine of the Imperium, its antibodies, fighting disease, insanity, injury, invasion.

I can think of no better way to serve, no better way to be an inquisitor.

So you have me then, pictured. Gregor Eisenhorn, inquisitor, puritan, Amalathian, forty-two years old standard, an inquisitor for the past eighteen years. I am tall and broad at the shoulders, strong, resolute. I have already told you of my force of will, and you will have noted my prowess with a blade.

What else is there? Am I clean-shaven? Yes! My eyes are dark, my hair darker and thick. These things matter little.

Come and let me show you how I killed Eyclone.

WATCHERS OF THE THRONE:

THE EMPEROR'S LEGION

CHRIS WRAIGHT

TIERON

I have considered it. Making an end to it all. Of course I have. I looked to the skies. I saw good souls succumb to weakness, and foul souls seize their moment.

What of it?

We all doubt.

I have lived over two hundred standard years. Too long, I think now. I have buried two wives, and seen seven children enter service and leave me for the void, and still I remain here, old, stubborn, in irritatingly good health despite an atmosphere of toxins both natural and political.

I am alone again now. Strange to say that, surrounded as I am by the quadrillions of the Throneworld, and yet it is truer now than it has ever been. The faces pass me by. I know all of them. I know their histories and their allegiances. I see the plots they hatch and hear the whispers they make under gilded archways, and I grow numb to it all, for it matters so little. Even now, hard against the End of Time, when the death rattle of our species has become audible even to the thick-eared, they still grasp for a little more of the things we have always desired – coin, power, knowledge, gratification.

We are yet animals, at heart. Nothing has changed that. Not even He could change us really, though I think He wanted to once. I like to believe that we must be a disappointment to Him. If we are not, then His ambitions for us must have been so very poor, and that strikes at all I believe and hold dear.

I am Alexei Lev Tieron, and I was a supremely power-ful man. I was not a warrior, nor was I a witch, nor was I a commander of great vessels. My power came only from the Lex Imperialis – a cold source, but an ancient one. Like so many within the bureaucracy that swathes us, I was pro-tected by words written on parchment. It gave me my station and defined it. Without this piece of paper, the meanest hive-ganger could have ended me with impunity – she would have ripped the jewels from my fingers and tried to sell them for weapons, and none would have come to my aid, for this galaxy only recognises strength.

But there are many kinds of strength. I learned this dur-ing schola, when I was as sickly as I am now hale, and the smooth-limbed scions of noble houses sought to crush my spirit with their brutishness. I might have died in that hateful place, had I not possessed the one talent that has preserved me ever since – the ability to deflect the ambition of oth-ers, to make it swerve, to direct hatred onto a target other than myself, to emerge from the lattice of competing egos intact and with no one aware of what veils have been cast over their stupid, powerful eyes.

No, I was not a witch. I just understood the pull of glory while having little attraction to it. I saw a man, or a woman, and I knew what they desired. I knew what to say to them, and I knew where to direct them. If they wished to do me harm, I found them prey more alluring. If they wished to help me, I extracted a suitable price. Thus I weaved my path between the paths of others, evading death while it devoured my rivals, until I reached the pinnacle, gazing back on a life of dissemblance and brokered deals. Compromise was my way, and for that I am despised, but that is as it should be. The Emperor has many servants, and we cannot all be power-armoured killers, can we?

I had many titles. This Imperium adores titles. The governor of the lowliest backwater rock will have a hundred names, each more ludicrous than the last. As for myself, only one really mattered: *Cancellarius Senatorum Imperialis*. Chancellor of the Imperial Council, in Low Gothic. Should you be inclined to trace that title back to its origins, you will find the true meaning of the words.

I was a doorkeeper. I watched people come and go. I made note of their intent, I had soft words with the ones who carried the weapons. I considered those who might be better suited to more exalted positions, and those who might be better extinguished. Over time, that capability generated a mix of terror and attraction. Many were afraid of what I could do to them; others speculated wildly on what I might desire, so that they might buy me and make me their creature. I was always amused by both reactions, for I did not act from malice and I cannot be bought. I was a cipher. Even now I wish for nothing other than that which I already possess, for I possess a very great deal.

I served in that station for nearly eighty years. I saw the composition of the High Twelve change over that span as death and rivalry took its toll. Some of those lords were vicious, many of them narcissists. Two were positively psychotic, and I remain convinced that a slim majority were always technically insane.

And yet – here's the thing – they were all quite superlative. You doubt this? You wish to believe that the masters of the Imperium are men and women of grasping inadequacy, forever squabbling over their own ambitions? Believe away. You're a fool.

There are twelve of them. Twelve. Consider what that means. More human souls now live than have ever lived. In the absence of the active guidance of He who sits on the Throne – may His name be blessed – it is those twelve alone who have guided our ravenously fecund species through ten thousand years of survival, within a universe that most assuredly desires to chew on our collective souls and spit the gristle out.

Many lesser mortals might have wished, in their idle moments, that they too could have risen to the heights, and sat on a throne of gold and ordered the Imperium as it ought to have been ordered – but they did not do it, and these ones did. They faced down the demands of the Inquisition, the belligerence of Chapter Masters, the condescension of mutant Novators and the injunctions of semi-feral assassins, and held their power intact. They orchestrated every response to every xenos incursion and patiently calibrated the defences of the Endless War. They withstood insurrections and civil strife, zealotry and madness. Every one of them is a master or mistress of the most strenuous and the most acute capability, though they burn out quickly – I have seen it – for the cares of humanity are infinite and they themselves are most assuredly finite.

So mock them if you will, and tell yourself that they have

fattened themselves on the labour of the masses and that they dwell in glorious ignorance while the galaxy smoulders to its inevitable ending. That is idiocy and it is indulgence. I served them for a good mortal span, judging them quietly even as they gave me their orders, and I tell you that though they had their many flaws, they were, and have always been, the greatest of us.

I never thought it would end. I never thought I would live to see the dawn of a day when the High Lords did not govern the Imperium as the highest arbiters of the Emperor's Will. In this, as in so much else, I have lived to see my error. Now, as I contemplate what must come next, I understand the true import of what I witnessed.

For the first time since He drew mortal breath, they no longer rule. For the first time since the Emperor was placed on the Holy Golden Throne, the High Lords no longer govern the Imperium that preserves His memory.

This is how it happened.

I remember the date. I remember the time, and remember the angle of the dying sun through my banqueting chamber's windows. You need not be detained with the figures, for all that has changed. In time, I suspect we will measure things from a different fulcrum, for they cannot remain as they were.

What is important? I do not know any more. My belly was full, as it was so often then. I was dining well from a table set with silver platters. All of it was real – fruits conveyed from the farthest reaches of the Segmentum in cryo-tanks. I felt the tight berries burst in my mouth as I chewed. One of those alone would have bought a hive spire on a lesser world, but we were on Terra, at the top of the pyramid, and barely gave it a thought.

Perhaps that offends you. Perhaps you think that we were insensitive to indulge ourselves at a time when so many wanted for the basic necessities of life.

I care nothing for your judgement. I care not for piety of any kind, and I do not regret the way we were then. We were sophisticates swimming in an infinity of resources, and we laboured for our luxuries. Above all, do not mistake indulgence for corruption – their elision is frequent but not inevitable, whatever some inquisitors might think.

I looked down the table, and saw the balance of power arranged at every place setting. The mighty were decked in their heavy gowns of office, weighed down with medallions and caskets. Their flesh was bronzed or black or gold, painted with the filigree of fine Martian improvements. They murmured to one another, keeping heads bowed so the words did not travel beyond the hearing of their present counterpart. They were accompanied by pleasure-companions – catamites, courtesans and confidantes, who were arrayed even more spectacularly in jerkins and gowns of silk and ruffs of lace. All skin was flawless, all eyes were bright, all conversation was fluid.

I held court, and enjoyed doing so. I saw the Lord Constable of the Synopticon lean in close to the neck of the Mistress Plenary of Catacombs and breathe something intended to be scandalous. She absorbed the information without reaction, which was little surprise, as she knew he was destined for removal in a week's time. She knew that because I had told her. She was the sponsor of the one who would replace him, so I judged it prudent to keep her informed, only asking for the standard level of discretion in return.

They were all at the same game, my guests – angling, jostling, manoeuvring – and that gave me no little pleasure, as they were all stepping, to a greater or lesser extent, to the moves I had given them.

I took another bite, then reached for a golden goblet of opalwine. My hands were heavy with silver, my arms draped with a cloak of thick velvet. Only as I drew the rim to my lips did I notice the presence hovering at my arm.

I had no servitors in my employ. I detest them, and even now will not admit them to my chambers. All my staff were human-normal, trained at the finest scholae and destined for positions of their own within the Adeptus Terra. This was one of those who had excelled – a student plucked from the Schola Havrath before he had turned fifteen standard, now my poison-catcher, his blood swimming with anti-toxins.

'Lord,' he whispered softly, lowering his head.

I turned to him. 'What is it, Galeas?'

'Forgive me. The Master awaits in your reception chamber.'

I did not need to ask which one. There were three Masters among the Twelve. The Master of the Astronomican, Leops Franck, would not have travelled here without warning, for he never went without an entourage of over a hundred attendants and that required planning; while the Master of the Administratum, Irthu Haemotalion, would not have deigned to visit me, but would have required me to visit him, such were the requirements of precedence that he set great store by. That left one: the Master of the Adeptus Astra Telepathica, Zlatad Aph Kerapliades.

My heart sank. I was enjoying myself. Kerapliades was a bore, a man atrophied by his work and shrivelled into a drab kernel of pessimism. If he had come here, it would be due to some dire portent delivered by his ranks of dream-speakers. The portents scryed by Kerapliades were always dire, and had been since his first blinded interpreter had been bound to the God-Emperor's holy will.

But he was a High Lord. If he was here, then I needed to be with him. I observed rank, for all my many sins – not even my many enemies ever accused me otherwise.

'Thank you,' I said to Galeas in the closed-speech of our household. 'Ensure he's comfortable – I will be there presently.'

I did not move immediately. Others would have observed Galeas leaving, and to follow him too swiftly would have invited speculation. I ate some more, I drank some more, I planted a seed of gossip in the mind of the Urbanius Cardinal of the Opheliate Tendency and exchanged pleasantries with a major general of the Astra Militarum segmentum command.

When the time was right, when the ebb and flow of the conversation had taken its own course, I rose from my seat and pulled my robes around me.

'You'll have to get along without me for a little while,' I said. 'Try not to eat everything, or each other, while I'm gone.'

Then I was out into the corridors, padding along the polished floors of my domain. I was dimly aware of movement in the shadows – my cadres of close protection bodyguards, hanging within las-shot range, tracking my every move. After so many years I barely noticed them, and even had they not been clad in cameleo-plate I might have forgotten they were there altogether.

My aide-de-camp Anna-Murza Jek fell in alongside me, her long gown whispering over the black marble.

'What's going on?' I asked, never breaking stride.

'He's flanked by his nulls,' she said, speaking quickly as she always did. 'That makes things difficult. This is a guess – he's worried about Cadia.'

'I'm worried about Cadia.'

'I don't have much else.'

'Run a grid-search over his senior staff movements.'

'Already under way.'

'How many of our people do we have in the Scholastia?'

'Thirty-seven.'

'Make contact with them all, and have reports in my chamber before dawn.'

'Already under way.'

I reached the doors to my reception chamber, turned to Jek and smiled. 'When you're done, have a drink.'

'If there's time, lord,' she said, bowing and withdrawing.

The doors opened.

My reception chamber was a wonderful place. It ought to have been – I had eighty years to refine it. The objects within it were the most exquisite, the decoration a study in good taste. On occasion, despite all the changes, I still spend time there, enjoying it. The High Lords have their own palaces, and the spires of the Senatorum are the most magnificent in the entire galaxy, but I still prefer the oasis I made there. It acts as the exemplar of the message I wished to send at all times – that we are more than guns and fury. We are an ancient species with subtle tastes. We are intelligent. And we are still here.

'My greetings, Master,' I said, closing the doors behind me.

Kerapliades was standing before a sandstone fireplace. He gave no indication he had any comprehension of how valuable it was – over twelve thousand years old, fashioned in pre-Unity Francia, literally irreplaceable – but I could not blame him for that. He spent his days in iron-ribbed spires determining how many thousands of human souls would be fed into the mechanisms of the Throne and how many hundreds would be doled out to lives of unremitting duty as sanctioned Imperial psykers. I might have been less than equable, had I been in his place.

'Is the chamber secure?' Kerapliades asked.

His long face, a bony white-grey with sunken black eyes, regarded me mournfully. He was nearly two metres tall, with high-bunched shoulders and long slender arms. His robes of office were simple – black, heavy fabric hanging in long swathes. He was flanked, as Jek had warned me, by his two nulls, whose psychic dampening aura was palpable even to me.

'All my chambers are secure, Master,' I said. 'You know this.'

'I know nothing any more.' Kerapliades leaned on a steel staff with an iron eye at its tip. 'I took a risk, coming here.'

He looked at me with rheumy eyes. I had never managed to find out just how much he could see through them. Almost all astropaths are blinded by their creation ritual, and those who retain some visual function are damaged in other ways, so they say. I never liked to speculate too closely on what his eyes must have seen since his own soul-binding.

'We speak in confidence,' I told him, and that was true. Anything told to me by one of the Council would never be disclosed to another unless they wished it to be.

Kerapliades limped away from the mantelpiece. There were chairs everywhere, but I knew he wouldn't sit.

'It's Cadia,' he said, as if that conveyed everything that needed to be said.

Well done, Jek, I thought.

For as long as the Imperium had existed, Cadia was ever at the forefront of its deliberations. Over the last two hundred years – my lifetime – the High Lords had devoted an ever-increasing amount of time to that one world. Regiments had been thrown into the void to bolster it. Space Marine Chapters had been petitioned to reinforce its approaches. Armour-wrights and strategeos had been seconded to augment its walls and its fortresses. There were other battle zones of import – Armageddon, Badab – in which we were stretched, but in truth none of them mattered besides Cadia, for if that world fell then the balance of power we had cultivated for ten thousand years would be ended at a stroke.

'You have tidings from the sector?' I asked.

'None.'

'Well then,' I said. 'In the absence of that–'

'You do not understand me.'

It was then that I first truly noticed the Master was not his moribund, desiccated self. I was used to seeing him gloomy. I was not used to seeing him scared. His long grey fingers clutched at his support, and even that did not quell the faint trembling.

'We can handle the visions,' he said, and he no longer looked at me. I do not think he was looking at anything in the chamber just then. 'I do not ask any of my alpha-level astropaths to undergo what I would not myself. I witness what they witness. I undergo the same trials.'

I let him speak. I will be truthful – his manner disturbed me. Kerapliades was not the confessional sort. I wondered if his mind had finally been cracked by the strain put on it, yet he did not show signs of mania, just a kind of dread.

'Probing that close to the Eye has always been perilous,' he went on. 'But now – nothing. No terror. No screaming visions. A curtain has been drawn across it.'

I did not know what to say to that. We had been at full-scale war over the Cadian Gate for over five years, and during that time we had relied on the Adeptus Astra Telepathica for the vast bulk of our knowledge of how our forces were faring. There had always been interference, and ambiguity, and often contradiction, but never silence. In my naivety I even wondered whether it might be a good thing – that the night-mares unleashed by our enemies there might be finally abating.

Then I looked at the Master again, and saw immediately that it was not a good thing.

'Tell me what you need,' I said.

'Need?' Kerapliades barked a dry sort of laugh. 'I need a thousand more psykers – stronger ones, not the dross I get from the Black Ships now.' He blinked. His breathing was shallow. 'This is different, chancellor. I can't read it yet, but my blood tells me true enough. Don't be misled by this calm – it comes before catastrophe.'

He had told me similar things before. I might have learned to ignore the warnings, if it were not for the horrendous expression on his mournful face.

'The Twelve must meet,' he said. 'And Dissolution must be enacted.'

So that was it. Another throw of this old die. Despite myself, my heart sank. The arguments had been scoured over and over for more years than I had been alive, and there had never been a resolution.

'I do not think that will be easy,' I said, already determining how such a thing could be done. '*Camera inferior* is not scheduled for another three months.'

Kerapliades whirled around, fixing me with his strange, swimming eyes. I felt a brief tremor, just for a moment – a flash of insight into his colossal psychic power. It was not meant as a threat, I think, just a momentary lapse in control, but the effect was still startling, like placing one's hand on static electricity.

'You can make it happen,' he said.

Possibly so. 'Have you spoken of this to any of the others?' I asked.

'None,' he said.

'Then I beg you – do not. Not yet. I will make my approaches – it would be best coming from me.'

'I know,' he said, and a grim smile cracked his features. 'You have wormed your way into the confidence of us all, doorkeeper. Sometimes I think you are the most dangerous man on Terra.'

Perhaps he meant that to be flattering.

'You give me too much credit,' I said. 'I merely accommodate.'

'So you say.' The hollow look in his eyes returned. 'Do it, though. Do what has to be done. If you need coin, if you need anything, let me know.'

That was an amusing thought. I had more coin than any of them knew. I could have bought half the Council with it already, were any of them remotely interested in such things, but, to their credit, none of them were. If they had vices then they were all connected to power, not avarice, and baubles held little sway over such souls.

'Of course, there is one difference, this time,' I ventured cautiously, knowing that I was telling Kerapliades something he already knew. 'The Lord Brach has not yet been replaced, and so one seat is empty.'

'Yes, and you know now what must be done, do you not?'

'I do not choose the High Lords,' I said.

'Go to see him,' he said.

'I do not think he will receive me,' I said.

'You will find a way,' he said.

And that was it. That was why he had come – to plant this idea in my head, to give it his blessing. I judged from this that he had support from others of the Twelve – he would not have advanced it if not. He was bound by the Lex Imperialis from making overt approaches himself, as were all his peers in the Council, but that would never stop them from making their views known.

It put me in a delicate position. Half the Council had always been against Dissolution, half for it. A reconfiguration might not change that, and by intervening now I risked aligning myself with a losing cause – a dangerous thing, even for a man like me.

I would need time to think. I would need time to confer with Jek and plot a route through this. The tides of intrigue in the Palace could rise fast and fall fast – the trick was not to be carried by them.

I bowed. 'I'm honoured that you came, Master,' I said.

Kerapliades did not return the bow.

'I'll be waiting,' he said, limping towards the chamber's doors. His nulls went with him, making my flesh crawl as they passed me.

Once he was gone, I waited awhile, pondering what to make of the visit. His fear had not been feigned. I still found it unsettling to witness fear from a High Lord, and that alone weighed more heavily on me than anything he had said.

After a suitable interval, Jek reappeared, looking curious. 'Anything of importance?' she asked.

'Not sure yet,' I said.

I was aware I had guests waiting. I placed my hands on Jek's to thank her for her concern, but could not linger to consult her then – that would have to wait for a few hours, by which point I might have settled the issues more clearly in my own mind.

I went back towards the dining chamber, gradually resuming my appearance of joviality as I walked. By the time I re-entered, my face was full of smiles again.

'What kept you?' asked the woman sitting on my left, just as the final courses were being delivered. 'Great matters of state?'

'A little indigestion,' I said, reaching for the sorbet. 'Not that there's much difference.'

YOUR
NEXT READ

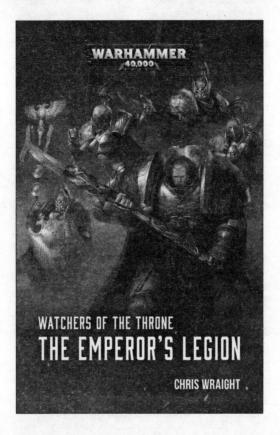

WATCHERS OF THE THRONE: THE EMPEROR'S LEGION
by Chris Wraight

The Adeptus Custodes are the Emperor's praetorian guard, the defenders of Terra and watchers over the Golden Throne. But when a threat arises, they and their Sisters of Silence allies may find themselves pressed almost beyond endurance…

FIRST AND ONLY

DAN ABNETT

PART ONE

The two Faustus-class Interceptors swept in low over a thousand slowly spinning tonnes of jade asteroid and decelerated to coasting velocity. Striated blurs of shift-speed light flickered off their gunmetal hulls. The saffron haze of the nebula called the Nubila Reach hung as a spread backdrop for them, a thousand light years wide, a hazy curtain which enfolded the edges of the Sabbat Worlds.

Each of these patrol Interceptors was an elegant barb about one hundred paces from jutting nose to raked tail. The Faustus were lean, powerful warships that looked like serrated cathedral spires with splayed flying buttresses at the rear to house the main thrusters. Their armoured flanks bore the Imperial eagle, together with the green markings and insignia of the Segmentum Pacificus Fleet.

Locked in the hydraulic arrestor struts of the command seat in the lead ship, Wing Captain Torten LaHain forced down his heart rate as the ship decelerated. Synchronous mind-impulse links bequeathed by the Adeptus Mechanicus hooked his meta-bolism to the ship's ancient systems, and he lived and breathed every nuance of its motion, power-output and response.

LaHain was a twenty-year veteran. He'd piloted Faustus Interceptors for so long, they seemed an extension of his body. He glanced down into the flight annex directly below and behind the command seat, where his observation officer was at work at the navigation station.

'Well?' he asked over the intercom.

The observer checked off his calculations against several glowing runes on the board. 'Steer five points starboard. The astropath's instructions are to sweep down the edge of the gas clouds for a final look, and then it's back to the fleet.'

Behind him, there was a murmur. The astropath, hunched in his small throne-cradle, stirred. Hundreds of filament leads linked the astropath's socket-encrusted skull to the massive sensory apparatus in the Faustus's belly. Each one was marked with a small, yellowing parchment label, inscribed with words LaHain didn't want to have to read. There was the cloying smell of incense and unguents.

'What did he say?' LaHain asked.

The observer shrugged. 'Who knows? Who wants to?' he said.

The astropath's brain was constantly surveying and processing the vast wave of astronomical data which the ship's sensors pumped into it, and psychically probing the warp beyond. Small patrol ships like this, with their astropathic cargo, were the early warning arm of the fleet. The work was hard on the psyker's mind, and the odd moan or grimace was commonplace. There had been worse. They'd gone through a nickel-rich asteroid field the previous week and the psyker had gone into spasms.

'Flight check,' LaHain said into the intercom.

'Tail turret, aye!' crackled back the servitor at the rear of the ship.

'Flight engineer ready, by the Emperor!' fuzzed the voice of the engine chamber.

LaHain signalled his wingman. 'Moselle... you run forward and begin the sweep. We'll lag a way behind you as a double-check. Then we'll pull for home.'

'Mark that,' the pilot of the other ship replied and his craft gunned forward, a sudden blur that left twinkling pearls in its wake.

LaHain was about to kick in behind when the voice of the astropath came over the link. It was rare for the man to speak to the rest of the crew.

'Captain... move to the following co-ordinates and hold. I am receiving a signal. A message... source unknown.'

LaHain did as he was instructed and the ship banked around, motors flaring in quick, white bursts. The observer swung all the sensor arrays to bear.

'What is this?' LaHain asked, impatient. Unscheduled manoeuvres off a carefully set patrol sweep did not sit comfortably with him.

The astropath took a moment to respond, clearing his throat. 'It is an astropathic communiqué, struggling to get through the warp. It is coming from extreme long range. I must gather it and relay it to Fleet Command.'

'Why?' LaHain asked. This was all too irregular.

'I sense it is secret. It is primary level intelligence. It is Vermilion level.'

There was a long pause, a silence aboard the small, slim craft broken only by the hum of the drive, the chatter of the displays and the whirr of the air-scrubbers.

'Vermilion...' LaHain breathed.

Vermilion was the highest clearance level used by the Crusade's cryptographers. It was unheard of, mythical. Even main battle schemes usually only warranted a Magenta. He felt an icy tightness in his wrists, a tremor in his heart.

Sympathetically, the Interceptor's reactor fibrillated. LaHain swallowed.

A routine day had just become very un-routine. He knew he had to commit everything to the correct and efficient recovery of this data.

'How long do you need?' he asked over the link.

Another pause. 'The ritual will take a few moments. Do not disturb me as I concentrate. I need as long as possible,' the astropath said. There was a phlegmy, strained edge to his voice. In a moment, that voice was murmuring a prayer. The air temperature in the cabin dropped perceptibly. Something, somewhere, sighed.

LaHain flexed his grip on the rudder stick, his skin turning to gooseflesh. He hated the witchcraft of the psykers. He could taste it in his mouth, bitter, sharp. Cold sweat beaded under his flight-mask. Hurry up! he thought... It was taking too long, they were idling and vulnerable; and he wanted his skin to stop crawling.

The astropath's murmured prayer continued. LaHain looked out of the canopy at the swathe of pinkish mist that folded away from him into the heart of the nebula a billion kilometres away. The cold, stabbing light of ancient suns slanted and shafted through it like dawn light on gossamer. Darkbellied clouds swirled in slow, silent blossoms.

'Contacts!' the observer yelled suddenly. 'Three! No, four! Fast as hell and coming straight in!'

LaHain snapped to attention. 'Angle and lead time?'

The observer rattled out a set of co-ordinates and LaHain steered the nose towards them. 'They're coming in fast!' the observer repeated. 'Throne of Earth, but they're moving!'

LaHain looked across his over-sweep board and saw the runic cursors flashing as they edged into the tactical grid.

'Defence system activated! Weapons to ready!' he barked. Drum autoloaders chattered in the chin turret forward of him as he armed the autocannons, and energy reservoirs whined as they powered up the main forward-firing plasma guns.

'Wing Two to Wing One!' Moselle's voice rasped over the long-range vox-caster. 'They're all over me! Break and run! Break and run in the name of the Emperor!'

The other Interceptor was coming at him at close to full thrust. LaHain's enhanced optics, amplified and linked via the canopy's systems, saw Moselle's ship while it was still a thousand kilometres away. Behind it, lazy and slow, came the vampiric shapes, the predatory ships of Chaos. Fire patterns winked in the russet darkness. Yellow traceries of venomous death.

Moselle's scream, abruptly ended, tore through the vox-cast.

The racing Interceptor disappeared in a rapidly expanding, superheated fireball. The three attackers thundered on through the fire wash.

'They're coming for us! Bring her about!' LaHain yelled and threw the Faustus round, gunning the engines. 'How much longer?' he bellowed at the astropath.

'The communiqué is received. I am now… relaying…' the astropath gasped, at the edge of his limits.

'Fast as you can! We have no time!' LaHain said.

The sleek fighting ship blinked forward, thrust-drive roaring blue heat. LaHain rejoiced at the singing of the engine in his blood. He was pushing the threshold tolerances of the ship. Amber alert sigils were lighting his display. LaHain was slowly being crushed into the cracked, ancient leather of his command chair.

In the tail turret, the gunner servitor traversed the twin auto-cannons, hunting for a target. He didn't see the attackers, but he saw their absence – the flickering darkness against the stars.

The turret guns screamed into life, blitzing out a scarlet-tinged, boiling stream of hypervelocity fire.

Indicators screamed shrill warnings in the cockpit. The enemy had obtained multiple target lock. Down below, the observer was bawling up at LaHain, demanding evasion procedures. Over the link, Flight Engineer Manus was yelling something about a stress-injection leak.

LaHain was serene. 'Is it done?' he asked the astropath calmly.

There was another long pause. The astropath was lolling weakly in his cradle. Near to death, his brain ruined by the trauma of the act, he murmured, 'It is finished.'

LaHain wrenched the Interceptor in a savage loop and presented himself to the pursuers with the massive forward plasma array and the nose guns blasting. He couldn't outrun them or outfight them, but by the Emperor he'd take at least one with him before he went.

The chin turret spat a thousand heavy bolter rounds a second. The plasma guns howled phosphorescent death into the void. One of the shadow-shapes exploded in a bright blister of flame, its shredded fuselage and mainframe splitting out, carried along by the burning, incandescent bow-wave of igniting propellant.

LaHain scored a second kill too. He ripped open the belly of another attacker, spilling its pressurised guts into the void.

It burst like a swollen balloon, spinning round under the shuddering impact and spewing its contents in a fire trail behind itself.

A second later, a rain of toxic and corrosive warheads, each a sliver of metal like a dirty needle, raked the Faustus end to end. They detonated the astropath's head and explosively atomised the observer out through the punctured hull. Another killed the flight engineer outright and destroyed the reactor interlock.

Two billiseconds after that, stress fractures shattered the Faustus class Interceptor like a glass bottle. A super-dense explosion boiled out from the core, vaporising the ship and LaHain with it.

The corona of the blast rippled out for eighty kilometres until it vanished in the nebula's haze.

GAUNT'S GHOSTS: THE FOUNDING
by Dan Abnett

The opening trilogy of the Gaunt's Ghosts saga returns! From the destruction of their world to their deadliest battle in the shattered hives of Verghast, this is the first act in the long-running fan favourite series.

FOR THE EMPEROR

SANDY MITCHELL

ONE

*'I don't know what effect they have on the enemy,
but by the Emperor, they frighten me.'*

– General Karis, of the Valhallans
under his command

One of the first things you learn as a commissar is that people are never pleased to see you; something that's no longer the case where I'm concerned, of course, now that my glorious and undeserved reputation precedes me wherever I go. A good rule of thumb in my younger days, but I'd never found myself staring down death in the eyes of the troopers I was supposed to be inspiring with loyalty to the Emperor before. In my early years as an occasionally loyal minion of his Glorious Majesty, I'd faced, or to be more accurate, ran away screaming from, orks, necrons, tyranids, and a severely hacked off daemonhost, just to pick out some of the highlights of my ignominious career. But standing in that mess

room, a heartbeat away from being ripped apart by muti-
nous Guardsmen, was a unique experience, and one that I
have no wish to repeat.

I should have realised how bad the situation was when the
commanding officer of my new regiment actually smiled at
me as I stepped off the shuttle. I already had every reason
to fear the worst, of course, but by that time I was out of
options. Paradoxical as it might seem, taking this miserable
assignment had looked uncomfortably like the best chance
I had of keeping my precious skin in one piece.

The problem, of course, was my undeserved reputation for
heroism, which by that time had grown to such ludicrous pro-
portions that the Commissariat had finally noticed me and
decided that my talents were being wasted in the artillery unit
I'd picked as the safest place to sit out my lifetime of service to
the Emperor, a long way away from the sharp end of combat.
Accordingly, I'd found myself plucked from a position of relative obscurity and attached directly to Brigade headquarters.

That hadn't seemed too bad at first, as I'd had little to do
except shuffle datafiles and organise the occasional firing
squad, which had suited me fine, but the trouble with everybody thinking you're a hero is that they tend to assume you
like being in mortal danger and go out of their way to provide
some. In the half-dozen years since my arrival, I'd been tem-
porarily seconded to units assigned, among other things, to
assault fixed positions, clear out a space hulk, and run recon
deep behind enemy lines. And every time I'd made it back
alive, due in no small part to my natural talent for diving for
cover and waiting for the noise to stop, the general staff had
patted me on the head, given me another commendation, and
tried to find an even more inventive way of getting me killed.

Something obviously had to be done, and done fast, before

my luck ran out altogether. So, as I often had before, I let my reputation do the work for me and put in a request for a transfer back to a regiment. Any regiment. By that time I just didn't care. Long experience had taught me that the opportunities for taking care of my own neck were much higher when I could pull rank on every officer around me.

'I just don't think I'm cut out for data shuffling,' I said apologetically to the weasel-faced little runt from the lord general's office. He nodded judiciously, and made a show of paging through my file.

'I can't say I'm surprised,' he said, in a slightly nasal whine. Although he tried to look cool and composed, his body language betrayed his excitement at being in the presence of a living legend; at least that's what some damn fool pictcast commentator had called me after the Siege of Perlia, and the appellation stuck. The next thing I know my own face is grinning at me from recruiting posters all over the sector, and I couldn't even grab a mug of recaf without having a piece of paper shoved under my nose with a request to autograph it. 'It doesn't suit everybody.'

'It's a shame we can't all have your dedication to the smooth running of the Imperium,' I said. He looked sharply at me for a moment, wondering if I was taking the frak, which of course I was, then decided I was simply being civil. I decided to ladle it on a bit. 'But I'm afraid I've been a soldier too long to start changing my habits now.'

That was the sort of thing Cain the Hero was supposed to say, of course, and weasel-face lapped it up. He took my transfer request from me as though it was a relic from one of the blessed saints.

'I'll handle it personally,' he said, practically bowing as he showed me out.

* * *

And so it was, a month or so later, I found myself in a shuttle approaching the hangar bay of the *Righteous Wrath*, a battered old troopship identical to thousands in Imperial service, almost all of which I sometimes think I've travelled on over the years. The familiar smell of shipboard air, stale, recycled, inextricably intertwined with rancid sweat, machine oil and boiled cabbage, hissed into the passenger compartment as the hatch seals opened. I inhaled it gratefully, as it displaced the no less familiar odour of Gunner Jurgen, my aide almost since the outset of my commissarial career nearly twenty years before.

Short for a Valhallan, Jurgen somehow managed to look awkward and out of place wherever he was, and in all our time together, I couldn't recall a single occasion on which he'd ever worn anything that appeared to fit properly. Though amiable enough in temperament, he seemed ill at ease with people, and, in turn, most preferred to avoid his company; a tendency no doubt exacerbated by the perpetual psoriasis that afflicted him, as well as his body odour, which, in all honesty, took quite a bit of getting used to.

Nevertheless he'd proven an able and valued aide, due in no small part to his peculiar mentality. Not overly bright, but eager to please and doggedly literal in his approach to following orders, he'd become a useful buffer between me and some of the more onerous aspects of my job. He never questioned anything I said or did, apparently convinced that it must be for the good of the Imperium in some way, which, given the occasionally discreditable activities I'd been known to indulge in, was a great deal more than I could have hoped for from any other trooper. Even after all this time I still find myself missing him on occasion.

So he was right there at my side, half-hidden by our combined luggage, which he'd somehow contrived to gather up and hold despite the weight, as my boot heels first rang on the deck plating beneath the shuttle. I didn't object; experience had taught me that it was a good idea for people meeting him for the first time to get the full picture in increments.

I paused fractionally for dramatic effect before striding forward to meet the small knot of Guard officers drawn up to greet me by the main cargo doors, the clang of my footsteps on the metal sounding as crisp and authoritative as I could contrive; an effect undercut slightly by the pops and clangs from the scorched area under the shuttle engines as it cooled, and Jurgen's tottering gait behind me.

'Welcome, commissar. This is a great honour.' A surprisingly young woman with red hair and blue eyes stepped forward and snapped a crisp salute with parade ground efficiency. I thought for a moment that I was being subtly snubbed with only the junior officers present, before I reconciled her face with the file picture in the briefing slate. I returned the salute.

'Colonel Kasteen.' I nodded an acknowledgement. Despite having no objection to being fawned over by young women in the normal course of events, I found such a transparent attempt at ingratiation a little nauseating. Then I got a good look at her hopeful expression and felt as though I'd stepped on a non-existent final stair. She was absolutely sincere. Emperor help me, they really were pleased to see me. Things must be even worse here than I'd imagined.

Just how bad they actually were I had yet to discover, but I already had some presentiment. For one thing, the palms of my hands were tingling, which always means there's trouble hanging in the air like the static before a storm, and for another, I'd broken with the habit of a lifetime and actually

read the briefing slate carefully on the tedious voyage out
here to meet the ship.

To cut a long story short, morale in the Valhallan 296th/301st
was at rock bottom, and the root cause of it all was obvious
from the regiment's title. Combining below-strength regiments was standard practice among the Imperial Guard, a
sensible way of consolidating after combat losses to keep
units up to strength and of further use in the field. What
hadn't been sensible was combining what was left of the
301st, a crack planetary assault unit with fifteen hundred
years of traditional belief in their innate superiority over
every other unit in the Guard, particularly the other Valhallan ones, with the 296th; a rear echelon garrison command,
which, just to throw promethium on the flames, was one of
the few all-women regiments raised and maintained by that
desolate iceball. And just to put the cherry on it, Kasteen had
been given overall command by virtue of three days' sen-
iority over her new immediate subordinate, a man with far
more combat experience.

Not that any of them truly lacked that now, after the battle
for Corania. The tyranids had attacked without warning, and
every Guard regiment on the planet had been forced to resist
ferociously for nearly a year before the navy and a couple of
Astartes Chapters[1] had arrived to turn the tide. By that time,
every surviving unit had sustained at least fifty per cent casualties, many of them a great deal more, and the bureaucrats
of the Munitorium had begun the process of consolidating
the battered survivors into useful units once again.

---

1 A common mistake. It is, of course, virtually unheard of for an entire Astartes
Chapter to take the field at once, let alone two; what Cain obviously means here
is that elements from two different Chapters were involved. (A couple of compa-
nies apiece from the Reclaimers and the Swords of the Emperor.)

On paper, at least. No one with any practical military experience would have been so half-witted as to ignore the morale effects of their decisions. But that's bureaucrats for you. Maybe if a few more Administratum drones were given lasguns and told to soldier alongside the troopers for a month or two it would shake their ideas up a bit. Assuming by some miracle they weren't shot in the back on the first day, of course.

But I'm digressing. I returned Kasteen's salute, noting as I did so the faint discolouration of the fabric beneath her rank insignia where her captain's studs had been before her recent unanticipated elevation to colonel. There had been few officers left in either regiment by the time the 'nids had got through with them, and they'd been lucky at that. At least one of the newly consolidated units was being led by a former corporal, or so I'd heard.[2] Unfortunately, neither of their commissars had survived so, thanks to my fortuitously timed transfer request, I'd been handed the job of sorting out the mess. Lucky me.

'Major Broklaw, my second-in-command.' Kasteen introduced the man next to her, his own insignia equally new. His face flushed almost imperceptibly, but he stepped forward to shake my hand with a firm grip. His eyes were flint grey beneath his dark fringe of hair, and he closed his hand a little too tightly, trying to gauge my strength. Two could play at that game, of course, and I had the advantage of a couple of augmetic fingers, so I returned the favour, smiling blandly as the colour drained from his face.

---

2 He'd heard wrong, or is possibly exaggerating for effect. The newly appointed colonel of the 112th Rough Riders was a former sergeant, true, but had already received a battlefield promotion to lieutenant during the defence of Corania. None of the senior command staff in any of the recently consolidated units had made the promotional jump directly from non-commissioned officer.

'Major.' I let him go before anything was damaged except his pride, and turned to the next officer in line. Kasteen had rounded up pretty much her entire senior command staff, as protocol demanded, but it was clear most of them weren't too sure about having me around. Only a few met my eyes, but the legend of Cain the Hero had arrived here before me, and the ones that did were obviously hoping I'd be able to turn round a situation they all patently felt had gone way beyond their own ability to deal with.

I don't know what the rest were thinking; they were probably just relieved I wasn't talking about shooting the lot of them and bringing in somebody competent. Of course, if that had been a realistic option I might have considered it, but I had an unwanted reputation for honesty and fairness to live up to, so that was that.

The introductions over I turned back to Kasteen, and indicated the tottering pile of kitbags behind me. Her eyes widened fractionally as she caught a glimpse of Jurgen's face behind the barricade, but I suppose anyone who'd gone hand to hand with tyranids would have found the experience relatively unperturbing, and she masked it quickly. Most of the assembled officers, I noted with well-concealed amusement, were now breathing shallowly through their mouths.

'My aide, Gunner First Class Ferik Jurgen,' I said. In truth there was only one grade of gunner, but I didn't expect they'd know that, and the small unofficial promotion would add to whatever kudos he got from being the aide of a commissar. Which in turn would reflect well on me. 'Perhaps you could assign him some quarters?'

'Of course.' She turned to one of the youngest lieutenants, a blonde girl of vaguely equine appearance who looked as if she'd be more at home on a farm somewhere than in uniform, and nodded. 'Sulla. Get the quartermaster to sort it out.'

'I'll do it myself,' she replied, slightly overdoing the eager young officer routine. 'Magil's doing his best, but he's not quite on top of the system yet.' Kasteen nodded blandly, unaware of any problem, but I could see Broklaw's jaw tighten, and noticed that most of the men present failed to mask their displeasure.

'Sulla was our quartermaster sergeant until the last round of promotions,' Kasteen explained. 'She knows the ship's resources better than anyone.'

'I'm sure she does,' I said diplomatically. 'And I'm sure she has far more pressing duties to perform than finding a bunk for Jurgen. We'll liaise with your Sergeant Magil ourselves, if you have no objection.'

'None at all.' Kasteen looked slightly puzzled for a moment, then dismissed it. Broklaw, I noticed from the corner of my eye, was looking at me with something approaching respect now. Well, that was something at least. But it was pretty clear I was going to have my work cut out to turn this divided and demoralised rabble into anything resembling a fighting unit.

Well, up to a point anyway. If they were a long way from being ready to fight the enemies of the Emperor, they were certainly in good enough shape to fight among themselves, as I was shortly to discover.

I haven't reached my second century by ignoring the little presentiments of trouble which sometimes appear out of nowhere, like those itching palms of mine, or the little voice in the back of my head which tells me something seems too good to be true. But in my first few days aboard the *Righteous Wrath* I had no need of such subtle promptings from my subconscious. Tension hung in the air of the corridors assigned to us like ozone around a daemonhost, all but striking sparks from the bulkheads. And I wasn't the only one to feel it. None of the other regiments on board would venture into our part of the ship, either for social interaction or the time-honoured tradition of perpetrating practical jokes against the members of another unit. The naval provosts patrolled in tense, wary groups. Desperate for some kind of respite, I even made courtesy calls on the other commissars aboard, but these were far from convivial; humourless Emperor-botherers to a man, the younger ones were too overwhelmed by respect for my reputation to be good company, and most of the older ones were quietly resentful of what they saw as a glory-hogging young upstart. Tedious as these interludes were, though, I was to be grateful for them sooner than I thought.

The one bright spot was Captain Parjita, who'd commanded the vessel for the past thirty years, and with whom I hit it off from our first dinner together. I'm sure he only invited me the first time because protocol demanded it, and perhaps out of curiosity to see what a Hero of the Imperium actually looked like in the flesh, but by the time we were halfway through the first course we were chatting away like old friends. I told a few outrageous lies about my past adventures, and he reciprocated with some anecdotes of his own, and by the time we'd got onto the amasec I felt more relaxed than I had in months. For one thing, he really appreciated the problems I was facing with Kasteen and her rabble.

'You need to reassert some discipline,' he told me unnecessarily. 'Before the rot spreads any further. Shoot a few, that'll buck their ideas up.'

Easy to say, of course, but not so easy in practice. That's

what most commissars would have done, admittedly, but getting a regiment united because they're terrified of you and hate your guts has its own drawbacks, particularly as you're going to find yourself in the middle of a battlefield with these people before very long, and they'll all have guns. And, as I've already said, I had a reputation to maintain, and a good part of that was keeping up the pretence that I actually gave a damn about the troopers under my command. So, not an option, unfortunately.

It was while I was on my way back to my quarters from one such pleasant evening that my hand was forced, and in a way I could well have done without.

It was the noise that alerted me at first, a gradually swelling babble of voices from the corridors leading to our section of the ship. My pleasantly reflective mood, enhanced by Parjita's amasec and a comfortable win over the regicide board, evaporated in an instant. I knew that sound all too well, and the clatter of boots on the deck behind me as a squad of provosts double-timed towards the disturbance with shock batons drawn was enough to confirm it. I picked up my pace to join them, falling in beside the section leader.

'Sounds like a riot,' I said. The blank-visored head nodded.

'Quite right, sir.'

'Any idea what sparked it?' Not that it mattered. The simmering resentment among the Valhallans was almost cause enough on its own. Any excuse would have done. If he did have a clue, I never got to hear it; as we arrived at the door of the mess hall a ceramic cup bearing the regimental crest of the 296th shattered against his helmet.

'Emperor's blood!' I ducked reflexively, taking cover behind the nearest piece of furniture to assess the situation while the provosts waded in ahead of me, striking out with their shock batons at any target that presented itself. The room was a heaving mass of angry men and women punching, kicking and flailing at one another, all semblance of discipline shot to hell. Several were down already, bleeding, screaming, being trampled on by the still active combatants, and the casualties were rising all the time.

The fiercest fighting was going on in the centre of the room, a small knot of brawlers clearly intent on actual murder unless someone intervened. Fine by me, that's what the provosts were for. I hunkered down behind an overturned table, scanning the room as I voxed a situation report to Kasteen, and watched them battle their way forward. The two fighters at the centre of the mêlée seemed evenly matched to me; a shaven-headed man, muscled like a Catachan, who towered over a wiry young woman with short-cropped raven black hair. Whatever advantage he had in strength she could match in agility, striking hard and leaping back out of range, reducing most of his strikes to glancing blows, which is just as well, as a clean hit from those ham-like fists would likely have stove her ribcage in. As I watched he spun, launching a lethal roundhouse kick to her temple; she ducked just a fraction slow, and went sprawling as his foot grazed the top of her head, but twisted upright again with a knife from one of the tables in her hand. The blow came up towards his sternum, but he blocked it, opening up a livid red gash along his right arm.

It was about then that things really started to go wrong. The provosts had made it almost halfway to the brawl I was watching when the two sides finally realised they had an enemy in common. A young woman, blood pouring from a broken nose, was unceremoniously yanked away from the man whose groin she'd been aiming a kick at, and rounded on the provost attempting to restrain her. Her elbow strike bounced harmlessly off his torso armour, but her erstwhile opponent leapt to her defence, swinging a broken plate in a short, clinical arc which impacted precisely on the neck joint where helmet met flak; a bright crimson spurt of arterial blood sprayed the surrounding bystanders as the stricken provost dropped to his knees, trying to stem the bleeding.

'Emperor's bowels!' I began to edge my way back towards the door, to wait for the reinforcements Kasteen had promised; if they hadn't been before, the mob was in a killing mood now, and anyone who looked like a symbol of authority would become an obvious target. Even as I watched, both factions turned on the provosts in their midst, who disappeared under a swarm of bodies. The troopers barely seemed human any more. I'd seen tyranids move like that in response to a perceived threat, but this was even worse. Your average 'nid swarm has purpose and intelligence behind everything it does, even though it's hard to remember that when a tidal wave of chitin is bearing down on you with every intention of reducing you to mincemeat, but it was clear that there was no intelligence working here, just sheer brute bloodlust. Emperor damn it, I've seen Khornate cults with more self-restraint than those supposedly disciplined Guard troopers displayed in that mess hall.

At least while they were ripping the provosts apart they weren't likely to notice me, so I made what progress I could towards the door, ready to take command of the reinforcements as soon as they arrived. And I would have made it too, if the squad leader hadn't surfaced long enough to scream, 'Commissar! Help!'

Oh great. Every pair of eyes in the room suddenly swung in my direction. I thought I could see my reflection in every pupil, tracking me like an auspex.

If you take one more step towards that door, I told myself, you're a dead man. They'd be on me in seconds. The only way to survive was to take them by surprise. So I stepped forward instead, as though I'd just entered the room.

'You.' I pointed at a random trooper. 'Get a broom.'

Whatever they'd been expecting me to say or do, this definitely wasn't it. The room hung suspended in confused anticipation, the silence stretching for an infinite second. No one moved.

'That was not a request,' I said, raising my voice a little, and taking another step forward. 'This mess hall is an absolute disgrace. And no one is leaving until it's been tidied up.' My boot skidded in a slowly congealing pool of blood. 'You, you, and you, go with him. Buckets and mops. Make sure you get enough to go round.'

Confusion and uncertainty began to spread, troopers flicking nervous glances at one other, as it gradually began to dawn on them that the situation had got well out of hand and that consequences had to be faced. The Guardsmen I'd pointed out, two of them women, began to edge nervously towards the door.

'At the double!' I barked suddenly, with my best parade-ground snap; the designated troopers scurried out, ingrained patterns of discipline reasserting themselves.

And that was enough. The thunderstorm crackle of violence dissipated from the room as though suddenly earthed.

After that it was easy; now that I'd asserted my authority the rest fell into line as meek as you please, and by the time Kasteen arrived with another squad of provosts in tow

I'd already detailed a few more to escort the wounded and worse to the infirmary. A surprising number were able to walk, but there were still far too many stretcher cases for my liking.

'You did well, I hear.' Kasteen was at my elbow, her face pale as she surveyed the damage. I shrugged, knowing from long experience that credit snowballs all the faster the less you seem to want it.

'Not well enough for some of these poor souls,' I said.

'Bravest thing I ever saw,' I heard from behind me, as one of the injured provosts was helped away by a couple of his shipmates. 'He just stood there and faced them down, the whole damn lot...' His voice faded, adding another small increment to my heroic reputation, which I knew would be all round the ship by this time tomorrow.

'There'll have to be an investigation.' Kasteen looked stunned, still not quite capable of taking in the full enormity of what had happened. 'We need to know who started it, what happened...'

'Who's to blame?' Broklaw cut in from the door. It was obvious from the direction of his gaze where he thought the responsibility should lie. Kasteen flushed.

'I've no doubt we'll discover the men responsible,' she said, a faint but perceptible stress on the pronoun. Broklaw refused to rise to the bait.

'We can all thank the Emperor we have an impartial adjudicator in the commissar here,' he said smoothly. 'I'm sure we can rely on him to sort it out.'

Thanks a lot, I thought. But he was right. And how I handled it was to determine the rest of my future with the regiment. Not to mention leaving me running for my life yet again, beginning a long and unwelcome association with the Emperor's pet psychopaths,[3] and an encounter with the most fascinating woman I've ever met.

---

3 *Not the most flattering or accurate description of His Divine Majesty's most holy Inquisition, it must be admitted.*

YOUR
NEXT READ

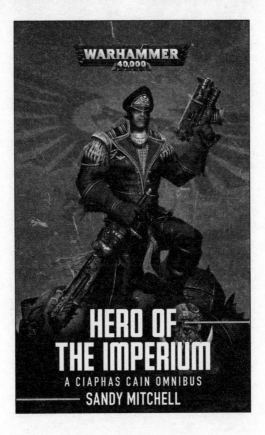

CIAPHAS CAIN: HERO OF THE IMPRERIUM
by Sandy Mitchell

In the 41st millennium Commissar Ciaphas Cain, hero of the Imperium, is an inspiration to his men – at least that's what the propaganda would have you believe…

HONOURBOUND

RACHEL HARRISON

ONE

Commissar Severina Raine slides a fresh magazine into her bolt pistol with a hard click. She has replaced the eight-round magazine four times. Thirty-two shots fired.

Six of them to execute her own troops.

Raine has fought many wars on many fronts across the Bale Stars, and almost all of them have been against the Sighted, or their splinter cults. She has seen the way they turn worlds with whispers and false promises. The way they set workers against their masters, and guards against those that they are meant to protect. It's what makes them dangerous. When you battle the Sighted, you battle the people of the Bale Stars too. Scribes and soldiers. Priests and peacekeepers. The poor, the downtrodden, the ambitious and the reckless. For some of those that serve with her, that knowledge is too much. For some it is just fear that means they find the trigger impossible to pull. No matter the reason, they will find themselves looking down the barrel of her pistol, Penance, in turn. Just like Penance, Raine is made for the act of judgement. For the instant before the strike of the hammer and the burst of flame. She understands what it means to pull the trigger, and what it makes her. She is not driven by anger, or malice. That would undermine her purpose, which is the same no matter the crime.

To eliminate weakness.

Raine crouches down and takes Jona Veer's ident-tags from around his neck. They will not be sent back to Antar as with the honoured dead. They will be disposed of at the end of the fight on Laxus Secundus. His name will go with them, to be forgotten in time by everyone but her, because Raine never forgets the dead, honoured or not.

'Commissar.'

The voice belongs to Captain Yuri Hale. It's rough-edged, like he is. The captain of Grey Company is tall, like most Antari. Three deep, severe scars run down the left side of his face from hairline to chin. The Antari call him lucky because he managed to keep his eye. They say he must have been graced with that luck by a white witch, or by fate itself. Raine doesn't believe in luck. She believes that Yuri Hale survives the same way the rest of them do.

By fighting for every breath.

'More power spikes from the inner forge,' he says.

Raine puts Veer's tags in her pocket, where they clatter against the others, then she gets to her feet and looks to the dust-caked screen on the auspex kit Hale is holding. When the regiment first entered the forges, more than six hours ago, it was registering soft spikes. Now the peaks are jagged, with the regularity of a great, slow heartbeat.

'Whatever the Sighted are doing in there, it's burning hot,' Hale says, and he frowns. 'Kayd's been picking up enemy vox too.'

'On an open channel?'

'Aye, it's as if they don't care if we hear it.'

'Anything of use?' Raine asks.

Hale's frown deepens, and it pulls at the scars on his face. 'The words were Laxian. Kayd reckons they said something like "it draws near".'

Despite the arid heat of the forge, Raine feels a distinct chill at those words. The tactical briefing two days prior had been clear. The primary forge on Laxus Secundus is an invaluable asset, both tactically and logistically, and not just because of the super-heavy tanks built there, but because of what waits in the inner forges. High Command did not disclose the purpose of the machines that Raine and the Antari would find there, only that they must not fall into Sighted hands. That for the enemy to use them success-fully would be catastrophic, not just for the battle inside the forges, but for the war effort across Laxus Secundus and the crusade front.

'We are running out of time,' Raine says.

Hale nods. 'And support too. Blue Company are pinned down on approach to the Beta Gate, and Gold have yet to reach the inner forges. I'm calling the push now, before the Sighted can send whatever *draws near* against us, or we lose everything we've bled for.'

'Understood, captain,' Raine says. 'We will not fail.'

Hale glances to where Jona Veer lies dead. Raine knows him well enough to see what he is feeling by the set of his shoulders, and the way his eyes narrow. Hale is disappointed. Ashamed, on the boy's behalf. Raine also knows that, despite all of Veer's failings, it is hard for Hale to accept judgement against one of his own.

'Is there anything else?' Raine says.

Hale looks back to her. 'No, commissar,' he says. 'Not a thing.'

Then Hale gets to rounding up the Antari, voxing orders to the rest of his company pushing up through the machine halls. They have orders to fulfil, traitors to silence, and those machines to retake.

And her judgements are something that Yuri Hale knows better than to question.

Lydia Zane can feel the touch of death on every inch of her body. It makes her ache, skin to bones. The Sighted are doing something in the forges that casts a long shadow. Something that echoes in the immaterium like a scream. It has been the same for Zane since the moment she set foot on Laxus Secundus, death's long shadow clinging to her.

Like that damned hateful bird.

It is sitting there now, talons crooked around the rim of a girder. It is so very still, that bird. She has not yet seen it blink. It never cries, or ruffles its feathers. It just sits still and stares.

On the pillar below the bird's perch is a symbol, daubed in blood. The smell carries to Zane even over the heavy stink of smoke. The symbol is a spiral surrounding a slit-pupilled eye. The mark of the Sighted. The rings of the spiral are just a hair off perfectly spaced, and it makes the breath in Zane's lungs thinner, looking at it. The Sighted who painted the symbol lies broken at the foot of the pillar. So very broken. He is clad in fatigues and feathers, his skin inked with iridescent, metallic tattoos. The Sighted was one of the flock hunting Jona Veer through the machine halls. Zane caught sight of him slipping into the shadows between the half-built tanks during the gunfight. He thought himself hidden, but he was wrong. There is no hiding from Zane, because she does not need footprints or line of sight or even sound in order to hunt. She followed him into the darkness by the stink of his traitor-thoughts and came upon him painting the spiral and the slitted eye.

And then she broke him.

Zane winds her fingers tighter around her darkwood staff. The psionic crystal atop it hums. One at a time, bolts pop out of the pillar and join the objects floating in the air around Zane. Tools. Rivets and screws. Empty shell casings. Splinters of bone. They drift around her absently. The floor tremors under her feet as the panels start to bend upwards. Zane tastes blood, running thick over her lips. Blood on the pillar. Blood that makes up the painted eye at the centre of the spiral, unblinking.

Just like the bird.

'Zane.'

She turns away from the bird and its black eyes and the way it never blinks them. Commissar Raine is standing there with her pistol drawn, but not raised. A threat in waiting. Zane finds she cannot speak. It is as if her lips have been sealed by all of that blood. The objects circle her like a storm, with lightning arcing between them. Raine does not flinch.

'Control,' Raine says, the word carrying clear.

The pistol does not move. The barrel is round and dark, like the eye painted in blood. Like the eyes of the bird. Like Raine's eyes, unblinking.

'Control,' Zane slurs.

More blood finds its way into her mouth.

'Tell me about the tree,' Raine says.

'About the tree,' Zane says, her voice a rasp. 'The singing tree.'

'And why is it called the singing tree?' Raine asks.

Zane blinks. Against the back of her eyelids she sees it. The singing tree standing on the cliff's edge, the roots curling over it like the bird's talons around the girder. The bone-white branches reaching up to meet Antar's thunderhead sky.

'Because that is where we would go to sing to Him on Earth,' she says. 'Because it was as close as you could get to the heavens.'

'And He spoke to you there,' Raine says.

'In the rustle of the leaves,' Zane says.

'What did He say?' Raine asks.

Zane feels the ache in her bones lessen. The objects orbiting her begin their fall to earth.

'That I will be tested,' she says. 'And that I must never break.'

Metal objects clatter off the metal floor, and it sounds like a storm.

'Lydia Zane,' Zane says, finishing the ritual words. 'Primaris psyker. Graded Epsilon. Eleventh Antari Rifles.'

The cables connecting to her scalp click as they cool. Zane wipes her hand through the blood on her face, painting a red streak up the back of it.

'Apologies, commissar,' she says, bowing low. 'It is this place. The darkness in it.'

'The Sighted?' Raine asks.

'I know the shape of their darkness,' Zane says. 'This is different. Things are changing.'

'If you see anything, tell me,' Raine says.

Zane knows that she means *foresee*, not just see, but it still feels like a cruel joke given the bird. The bird that she has been seeing for months now, since she walked the crystal tunnels on Gholl. The bird that she will speak of to no one, especially not to Raine, because to do so would be to invite death.

Because Zane knows that, like every instant of her life so far, the bird is just another test, and that she will not break.

Sergeant Daven Wyck waits until the commissar has gone after the witch before he fetches Jona Veer's rifle. He knows better than to do something like that in front of her. That it's better not to draw her eyes at all if he can help it. Around him, the rest of his Wyldfolk are securing the area at the end of the assembly line, watching for Sighted movement in the smoke. They tend their rifles and replace spent powercells and share out grenades and charges. Clean their bloodied combat blades on their fatigues. Wyck slings Veer's rifle over his shoulder by the strap, then takes his knife and his grenades too. Veer hadn't used even one of them. So stupid, not to shoot, or act at all.

Even more so to get found out.

'Really, Dav?' Awd says.

Wyck gives his second a look. The sort that says *shut up*.

'He isn't going to use them, is he?' he says.

Awd looks as though he's smiling, but it's just the way the burn scars tug at the skin of his face. His eyes aren't smiling at all.

'You'd truly leave him with nothing for where he's going?' Awd asks.

Wyck looks down at Veer's body and remembers the way he spoke, with that lilt of the Vales. It's the same place that Wyck grew up before he was tithed to the Rifles, all deep black lakes and tangled forests. It's a big place, with the people spread thin. Wyck didn't know Veer then. He didn't know him now either, not really, but he was kin all the same. Even if he was a coward, and a stupid one at that. Wyck stoops and puts back the knife. Awd's right. He can't leave Veer with nothing for when judgement comes.

'There,' he says. 'Now it's up to him to answer for his deeds.'

Awd nods. 'As we all will, in death.'

Wyck shakes his head. 'Death will have to catch me first,' he says.

That makes Awd laugh so hard he starts to cough, a wet hacking sound from deep in his chest. It's the flamer he carries that makes his lungs rattle that way. All the ashes from the fuel and the things he burns.

'Death will have to be lucky,' Awd says. 'Sharp soul like you.'

Wyck smiles, but it doesn't go deeper than his teeth. He curls his hands into fists. They ache from fighting. From every trigger pull, every swipe of the knife. From throwing punches and breaking bones. That ache doesn't stop him wanting to fight, though. To cut and shoot and kill. If anything, it makes him want it more.

'Wyck.'

He turns to see Hale standing there. The captain definitely notices the extra lasrifle and the grenades, but he says nothing about either. Wyck has known Hale a long time. Longer than he's had to call him captain.

'We are pushing the Gate,' Hale says. 'I need your Wyld-folk up front.'

The order is no surprise. Wyck runs his twelve-strong infantry squad fast and sharp, so Hale always puts them in the teeth of it.

'Aye, sir,' Wyck says. 'I wouldn't be anywhere else.'

Hale claps him on the shoulder and for the sparest instant Wyck's instinct is to react as if he's been hit. He has to consciously stop himself from throwing a punch at his captain and force himself into stillness. It's the adrenaline, mostly.

'Fire and thunder,' Hale says.

Wyck thinks about the way his blood burns and his heartbeat rolls like a drum and the old words seem almost funny. He has to stop himself laughing, just like he had to stop himself throwing that punch.

'Fire and thunder,' he says, instead.

It takes Raine and the Antari another hour to fight their way from the assembly lines into the casting halls. The colossal, vaulted chambers are the midpoint of the forge complex, and the most direct path to the forge halls and the Delta Gate beyond. Like the rest of the Forge Primary, the casting halls are still working unabated despite the conflict taking place across the complex. All around Raine, vast machines judder and roar. Overhead, great buckets of molten steel are raised by lifters and poured, spitting, into the moulds beneath. Censers swing over the moulds, and slaved cherubim drop ritual ashes, still running on subroutines that were set long before the war began. The panels move down the line to be beaten, quenched and cooled by blasts of dirty water, filling the halls with smoke, steam and the smell of industry.

To Raine, it feels like running through hell. It makes her long for the icy, ocean-spray winters of Gloam, where she was trained. For clothes stiff with frost, and for the misting of breath in the air.

The casting halls are occupied by dug-in squads of Sighted infantry. Most of them are sworn rebels and traitors that wear blue and grey flak plate and the trappings of heretics. Mirrored glass on bits of cord. Feathers that pierce their skin. The spiral-eye symbol, daubed in red. The rest are faith-breakers, a mixture of manufactorum workers, tech-savants and defected Laxian soldiery that have torn away their icons and excised their loyalty tattoos. Raine cannot say which disgusts her more, but no matter the nature of their betrayal, they will all be granted the same fate.

Death.

'Leave none standing!' she cries, as she charges into combat alongside the Antari.

One of the Sighted looms from the steam and smoke. His eyes are solid black, and his teeth are filed to sharp points. Heretic sigils run and bleed on the Sighted's flak armour, and the heavy, two-handed sword he carries seems to swallow what little light there is. Raine dodges him as he swings for her with that heavy blade. It could take her head clean off if it were to hit her, but the Sighted plants it in the riveted metal of the floor instead, where it sticks for an instant.

An instant is all Raine needs.

She opens the Sighted up from belt to throat with an upward swing of her own powered blade. As he falls, she fires her pistol past him, knocking another of the heretics to the ground in a burst of blood. Behind him, there are more. Dozens more. Hale is right beside her, his laspistol drawn. It's a heavy variant with warding words carved into the grip in Antari script. One sleeve of his fatigues is torn and smoking where las-fire has caught him, and his flak armour has been scored by a dozen blades.

'They are different,' Hale says, between breaths. 'They have always had numbers, and ferocity, but this is more than that. They are well-armed. Organised.'

Raine fires her pistol as the Sighted fall back towards their own lines and the cover of the forge machinery. They are doing it in good order, under smoke. Some carry slab shields, protecting those beside and behind them, making a mobile defensive line. On Drast, they fought her as if their minds were lost, until they had no limbs left to do it with. They dropped their rifles in favour of knives, because they placed more value on blood than survival. They were dangerous, but they were feral, and fractious. Zane's words echo in Raine's ears.

Things are changing.

'You are right,' she says to Hale. 'But we will kill them all the same.'

Hale nods, and speaks his next words into the company vox-channel.

'All squads advance,' he says. 'We break them as they run!'

Raine raises her sword. Misted water from the machinery hisses on Evenfall's powered blade. 'Give them death,' she shouts. 'In the Emperor's name!'

The Antari of Grey Company cheer. The Hartkin. The Mist-vypers. The Pyrehawks. The ones to cheer the loudest are those right beside her in the teeth of it. Wyck's Wyldfolk. They are leading the push, like always. Hale uses Wyck as a blade's edge, because it is what he is good for.

'Yulia!' Wyck shouts. 'Deal with those shields!'

Yulia Crys grins and unslings her grenade launcher. Raine takes cover in the shadow of a casting machine for the moment it fires. The noise of it is like thunder, a series of rapid, automatic thumps that puts half a dozen grenades in the Sighted's lines, in and around those slab shields. They detonate almost immediately. Raine can't see the damage for all the smoke and the fire, but she hears it. The crack of armour and bone. Screams. The scattering of debris landing around her.

'What shields, sarge?' Crys shouts.

Wyck laughs. It is an unpleasant sound.

'Keep pushing forward!' Raine shouts.

The breath she takes tastes of ash and smoke, and blood too. The Sighted that Crys' grenades didn't kill are running now, much less ordered. Raine fires Penance twice, putting two of them down with quick kill shots. The Wyldfolk light the casting halls with bright flashes of las-fire all around her. The tide has turned. The Sighted are faltering. Dying. But then Raine is hit by a heavy calibre round that impacts against her silver chest-plate and puts a fist-sized dent in it. It knocks the air from her lungs and cracks something in her chest, knocking her aim out. Raine's vision swims, but she catches sight of the Sighted who shot her. He is a tall, whipcord-thin man wearing blue-grey carapace with a cut stone replacing one of his eyes. It is a mark of rank on them, a stone like that. He raises his snub-nosed shotgun to fire again and smiles. Raine raises her pistol, but before she can pull the trigger Wyck slams into the Sighted and knocks him onto his back. Raine hears the shotgun go off. Hears Wyck laugh. She makes an effort to breathe until it isn't agony to do it. The Wyldfolk have the other Sighted dead or running. She makes her way to where Wyck is kneeling. The Sighted underneath him is a mess. His throat is open and pumping blood all over the floor.

'Too slow,' Wyck says, softly. 'Much too slow.'

'Enough,' Raine says to him. 'On your feet.'

He looks up at her. For an instant, there's no recognition in those grey eyes of his. Barely any grey either. It's all swallowed up by the black of his pupils. But then he blinks and takes a ragged breath.

'Enough,' he says, getting to his feet. 'Yes, commissar.'

His voice is deliberate and careful. His use of her rank even more so. Wyck often cloaks himself in obedience and piety when he is being watched.

'He said something,' Wyck says. 'That we can't kill the life they will make here.'

The words, and the implication of them, turn Raine's stomach. She knows what the Sighted are capable of. She has seen it first hand, on Gholl and Drast, and all of the worlds before them. Devastation, and desecration. Whole populations sacrificed in rites and rituals. Blood spilt on a massive scale, all in the name of their false prophets.

And now the Sighted intend to *make life*.

Whether it is soldiers or slaves, or something worse, Raine cannot allow it.

'Whatever it is that they intend, we will stop them,' she says. 'At any cost.'

Raine thinks then of the machines that the Antari have been charged with capturing. Those that would cause catastrophe if the enemy were to use them.

Here, and across the crusade front.

Wyck flinches and turns to look up the avenue, towards the Sighted's lines, where the traitor infantry disappear into the smoke and steam.

'There's something coming,' he says. 'Something heavy.'

Raine strains her ears over the sounds of the casting machines and then she hears it too. Heavy, clanking footsteps.

'Make ready!' she shouts.

The rest of Grey Company have caught up to them now. They take what cover they can behind the casting machines and reload their rifles and pistols. Water spray from the machines runs off the brim of Raine's hat, mingling with the sweat in her eyes. Steam rolls across the avenue like ocean fog.

Through it stride three armoured shapes, half as tall again as the tallest of the Antari. They have domed heads and heavy fists that end in blaster weapons. Carapace-mounted flame-throwers track back and forth on their shoulders. The kastelan automata are stripped back to bare steel, save for the great red spirals painted on their domed heads. At the centre of each is a slit-pupiled eye. With them moves a figure that is human only in shape, dribbling oil onto the forge floor from beneath its black robes. Mechadendrites thrash at its back. The tech-priest turns its face to the Antari, to Raine, and it blares machine noise from the grille of its mouth.

'Pyrehawks!' Captain Hale shouts.

All of the Rifles' infantry squads are named for Antari folk stories, and Raine has come to know most of them since joining the regiment. Andren Fel told Raine that the pyre-hawk was said to be the one to light Antar's night sky with stars, setting hundreds of fires in the void with every beat of its wings.

Raine cannot think of a more appropriate name for Kasia Elys and her five-strong special weapons team. They are heavily armoured, with extra plates strapped around their arms and legs, and glare visors in their helmets. The Pyrehawks move up into position and brace their plasma guns, ready to light new stars.

'Set them afire,' Elys snarls.

The Pyrehawks fire their plasma guns in the same instant as the kastelans do their phosphor blasters. Bright white light blooms in the casting halls, printing on Raine's eyes. She is half-blind as she fires her pistol at the kastelan automata and the tech-priest controlling them.

One of Odi's Hartkin is hit by phosphor. Raine can't say who, because there is not enough left to know. The figure is silently running towards the rest of its squad in its blind death throes. Raine puts a bolt in the figure to stop it from passing the phosphor along to the rest of them. It falls, still burning.

In return, one of the kastelans goes to a knee, juddering and smoking from plasma fire. The tech-priest is blaring more machine noise that sounds like a scream. The other two kastelans twist and train their phosphor cannons at Elys and her Pyrehawks as they go for cover. The Pyrehawks fire again as they fall back, trading plasma for phosphor. Their shots land true, staggering the kastelans, but not felling them. Most of the Pyrehawks end up burning like stars themselves and Raine doesn't have enough rounds for all of them.

Not if she wants to kill the tech-priest.

'Zane!' she shouts.

There is no way the psyker hears her over all of the noise, not really. But Zane does not need to truly hear.

'The kastelans!' Raine shouts. 'Break them!'

Lydia Zane walks through the storm as dozens of her kin fall back, firing at the kastelans. One of the automata moves to meet her and the flamethrower on its shoulder angles downwards. Zane raises her hand as the kastelan fires a gout of promethium that would melt her like the steel in the forge if it were to touch her skin. Instead, Zane deflects the liquid flame back over the kastelan in an arc. She feels the heat of it against her kine-shield as a fire in her mind. The cables at her skull creak and the floor under her feet trembles and twists. The kastelan, burning now, reaches for her with a huge, powered fist. For an instant, Zane almost pities the machine. This thing that is made to take commands, and never to question. Only to kill. She sees herself reflected in the mirror of its faceplate. Her nose is bleeding thickly, and her skin is as pale as a lakebottom fish. The crown of cables that thread under her scalp are arcing with lightning.

'Die,' Zane says, and throws up her hand.

The kastelan robot explodes into pieces, disassembled in an instant, all bolts sheared, all seals broken. The floor panels around Zane splinter. Dozens of metres away, overhead cables flex and snap. The shockwave knocks some of her kin to the ground, breaking bones. She hears them scream. The world wavers, and time seems to slow. Zane's heart goes arrhythmic and she distinctly hears the snap of folding wings. She wishes that closing her eyes would stop it, but it never does. Especially not since she lost her real eyes, and had them replaced with false silver discs. Now she sees fire and death in every blink.

It is a test, she thinks. *And I will not break.*

With a scream of effort, Zane refocuses, and turns to the last remaining kastelan and its tech-priest overseer. The tech-priest is slowly raising its arm. Its gamma pistol is pointed at Raine. The commissar's own pistol is raised in answer, but even one as quick as Raine will be ashes if fire from the tech-priest's weapon so much as grazes her. Lydia Zane does not care for the commissar. The psyker is not a hound, loyal and loving to her master. She is caged and tethered, watched and judged, all by Raine. But if Lydia Zane is truly honest, she is sometimes thankful for the strength of this particular tether.

So Zane lifts her hand and curls it into a fist as the tech-priest's fingers ratchet around the gamma pistol's trigger. She turns the gun to scrap, along with most of the priest's arm. It shrieks and rears back. The last kastelan stumbles forwards on jarred, broken legs, still slaved to protect its master. Zane squeezes it with invisible force until the joints burst and it collapses, crushed. Exhausted, Zane falls to her knees, with electricity dancing from the cables of her crown and running along her teeth.

On Gloam, where she was trained, they would make Raine run the upper gantries over the ocean. They were narrow spans of riveted metal, either slick with sea-spray or with ice when it turned to deepwinter. The trick was to run quickly and surely. Second guess yourself, and the ocean would gladly take you. Raine places her feet just as surely, just as swiftly, as she leaps up on the fallen kastelan's shell and snaps off the last three rounds of her bolt pistol's magazine. They all hit the tech-priest. Chest, throat. Head. It falls backwards, thrashing, the bladed mechadendrites seeking her. Her pistol empty, Raine draws her sabre. Evenfall's power field snarls. One of the tech-priest's mechadendrites cuts Raine's face as another tears a great rip in her greatcoat and her arm. Raine feels blood run hot and fast as she swings her sabre, severing the mechanical arms as they reach for her, until she is close enough to plant the powered blade in the tech-priest's chest. Even then, it takes a moment to stop twitching.

Raine draws a breath, all ashes and the smell of spilled oil. The Sighted have all but disappeared into the smoke, taking cover in amongst the vast casting machines standing between the Antari and the forge halls beyond. Raine pushes another magazine into her pistol. She is down to her last two.

'No respite!' she cries. 'No mercy!'

And around her, the Antari roar and push onwards.

Wyck falls back against one of the casting machines. At his feet, the Sighted takes his time to die, bleeding out slowly across the corrugated floor. The smell of it dizzies Wyck as he cleans the blade of his knife on the leg of his fatigues. Everything seems muffled as if by distance. The thrum of the machine at his back. The las-fire echoing up to the roof.

The Sighted at his feet, choking to death.

Wyck blinks his stinging eyes. He looks back down the aisle to make sure he is still alone before putting his hand in the pouch at his belt and taking out a short, stubby vial with an auto-injector mounted on the cap. Wyck breaks the seal with his thumb, and then punches the needle into his arm, straight through his fatigues. The rush comes quickly, like it always does. Setting him alight from the inside out. Sounds go from murmurs to bellows and everything pulls pin sharp.

Wyck drops the auto-injector on the floor and crushes it with his boot.

'The way is clear,' he says, into the vox. 'Move up.'

His Wyldfolk approach up the aisle, resolving as if from the smoke and the darkness, their green and grey flak plate fouled with ashes and blood.

'I don't like this, sarge,' Crys says. 'We're way out in it.'

The combat engineer is twitching her head from side to side, trying to compensate for the fact she's part-deaf in her left ear. Crys is taller than he is, and so broad across the shoulders that standard template flak plate doesn't fit her all that well. She has her grenade launcher slung across her back and her pistol drawn in its place. Crys has modified the grenade launcher, like she does all of her kit. It's something that she should be sanctioned for, but Wyck has seen how that gun works since. What it can do. The box and cabling mounted on the stock of it increase the speed of the rotary magazine, so that it fires on full auto.

By all rights, Yulia Crys should be deaf in both of her ears.

'We're always way out in it,' Wyck says. 'It's what we're good at.'

Crys shrugs her broad shoulders, but she's still frowning. In some ways, she's right. They are deep into the labyrinth of casting machines, probably cut off from the rest of Grey, but Wyck has the Sighted running and he won't stop chasing until he's bled the lot of them.

Wyck takes point, following after a sound he picks up even over the machines and the gunfire. The ring of boots on metal. He rounds a corner and follows a set of bare plated stairs upwards. It brings him out on top of a rig mounted with plasma torches that are cutting shapes from huge sheets of steel. He moves up the central gantry with his squad behind him. It is noisy, with equally spaced alcoves like confessionals arranged on either side for the machine's slaved servitors. A lot of cover, for those who might hide. Sparks rain from the machines, and smoke blows across the gantry like fog.

No good, Wyck thinks. *This is no good.*

The servitors loll at their stations, operating the torches with convulsive movements of their withered limbs. They don't look up as Wyck passes because their routines don't allow it. Because they are made for the moment of the cut and nothing more. Wyck's fingers twitch by the trigger. The stimms are pressing at him and are making him shake, just minutely.

There's a noise. The barest sound that he wouldn't be able to pick up if his brain weren't so electric.

One of the Sighted lurches out of the next alcove on his left. No carapace on this one. No flak armour. The man is clad in coveralls and he has a heavy, long-handled hammer in his hand. He swings for Wyck, but he is much too slow. Wyck ducks the swing and puts his boot in the man's gut, sending him reeling. He snaps three las-rounds into him before he can get back up again.

More of them come, out of the alcoves, or dropping from ledges above. A dozen or so. They are shouting something over the noise in Laxian. Two of them are down and twitching from chest shots before they can pull their weapons. The sound of them gasping for air they can't get carries to him even as Wyck puts his knife in the chest of a third. He pulls it free again, but the Sighted doesn't go down. Instead he coughs blood onto Wyck's face and swings for him, raking a blunt-edged knife across the front of Wyck's flak armour. It digs a gouge, but doesn't go through. Wyck blinks the blood from his eyes. He can't help but laugh.

'You think you can cut me?' he says.

Wyck cuts the Sighted back, across his arms as he tries to block, then across his throat when his arms finally drop. Wyck gets more blood on his face. His heart is so loud now. Louder than the las-fire and the roaring of Awd's flamer as they finish the rest of them.

'I'm Wyldfolk,' Wyck says. 'And cuts from us always kill.'

'Dav.'

For a moment, Wyck could swear it's Raf's voice he hears, after all this time. There's the same kind of dread in it.

'Dav.'

Wyck blinks and shakes his head. Of course it's not Raf. Raf has been dead for more than ten years. Long since taken. Long since judged. He turns to see Awd looking at him. The others are moving swiftly up the gantry, checking for runners or trip mines.

'What?' Wyck asks.

'These folk,' Awd says, slow and careful. Quiet. 'I don't think they're Sighted.'

Wyck snorts. 'What are you talking about?' he says.

He looks at the body at his feet. The pool of blood that has spread around his boots like a black lake. Wyck realises that the man hasn't cut up his face or torn away his icons. He wears no mirrors or feathers, and his coveralls are Munitorum-issue. The only mark on the man is the worker number branded on his neck. It occurs to Wyck that the blunt-bladed knife is the sort you'd use to pry panels off machines.

'They were behind the lines,' Wyck says, absently. 'They jumped us.'

'I found this on one of them,' Awd says.

He throws something that Wyck catches. Something shiny and silver. No, not silver. Tin. Cheaply pressed.

It's a pendant in the shape of the aquila.

The thunder of Wyck's heart skips a beat. In his head, he hears what Raf said to him, all those years ago, his grey eyes wide with horror.

What have you done, Dav?

The answer is the same now as it was then.

Too much to forgive.

Wyck blinks and clears his throat. 'You know how they are,' he says to Awd. 'The Sighted make soldiers of everyone, even if they don't look like it. They did it on Gholl. On Hyxx too. Even the priests, there. You remember?'

'I remember,' Awd says. 'I won't forget that. Not even when I'm dead.'

'Everywhere they go, people turn their coats for them. This is just that.'

Wyck puts the pendant in one of the pouches at his belt. The one next to where he keeps the auto-injectors.

'I know,' Awd says. 'But–'

Wyck gives him that look again, and just like before, Awd falls silent.

'This is just that,' he says again. 'Now forget it and move.'

Awd nods his head. 'Yes, sergeant. As you say.'

Wyck glances down at the body one more time before following Awd. At the blunt-bladed knife and the wide pool of blood. At the aquila pendant glinting around that man's neck too.

And he knows that when death finally catches him, he'll have so very much to be judged for.

YOUR
NEXT READ

HONOURBOUND
by Rachel Harrison

Commissar Severina Raine and the 11th Antari Rifles fight to subdue the spreading threat of Chaos burning across the Bale Stars. Little does Raine realise the key to victory lies in her own past, and in the ghosts that she carries with her.

THE HORUS HERESY®

HORUS RISING

DAN ABNETT

ONE

BLOOD FROM MISUNDERSTANDING

OUR BRETHREN IN IGNORANCE

THE EMPEROR DIES

'I was there,' he would say afterwards, until afterwards became a time quite devoid of laughter. 'I was there, the day Horus slew the Emperor.' It was a delicious conceit, and his comrades would chuckle at the sheer treason of it.

The story was a good one. Torgaddon would usually be the one to cajole him into telling it, for Torgaddon was the joker, a man of mighty laughter and idiot tricks. And Loken would tell it again, a tale rehearsed through so many retellings, it almost told itself.

Loken was always careful to make sure his audience properly understood the irony in his story. It was likely that he felt some shame about his complicity in the matter itself, for it was a case of blood spilled from misunderstanding. There was a great tragedy implicit in the tale of the Emperor's murder, a tragedy that Loken always wanted his listeners to appreciate. But the death of Sejanus was usually all that fixed their attentions.

That, and the punchline.

It had been, as far as the warp-dilated horologs could attest, the two hundred and third year of the Great Crusade. Loken always set his story in its proper time and place. The commander had been Warmaster for about a year, since the triumphant conclusion of the Ullanor campaign, and he was anxious to prove his new-found status, particularly in the eyes of his brothers.

Warmaster. Such a title. The fit was still new and unnatural, not yet worn in.

It was a strange time to be abroad amongst stars. They had been doing what they had been doing for two centuries, but now it felt unfamiliar. It was a start of things. And an ending too.

The ships of the 63rd Expedition came upon the Imperium by chance. A sudden etheric storm, later declared providential by Maloghurst, forced a route alteration, and they translated into the edges of a system comprising nine worlds.

Nine worlds, circling a yellow sun.

Detecting the shoal of rugged expedition warships on station at the out-system edges, the Emperor first demanded to know their occupation and agenda. Then he painstakingly corrected what he saw as the multifarious errors in their response.

Then he demanded fealty.

He was, he explained, the Emperor of Mankind. He had stoically shepherded his people through the miserable epoch of warp storms, through the Age of Strife, staunchly maintaining the rule and law of man. This had been expected of him, he declared. He had kept the flame of human culture alight through the aching isolation of Old Night. He had sustained this precious, vital fragment, and kept it intact, until such time as the scattered diaspora of humanity re-established contact. He rejoiced that such a time was now at hand. His soul leapt to see the orphan ships returning to the heart of the Imperium. Everything was ready and waiting. Everything had been preserved. The orphans would be embraced to his bosom, and then the Great Scheme of rebuilding would begin, and the Imperium of Mankind would stretch itself out again across the stars, as was its birthright.

As soon as they showed him proper fealty. As Emperor. Of mankind.

The commander, quite entertained by all accounts, sent Hastur Sejanus to meet with the Emperor and deliver greeting.

Sejanus was the commander's favourite. Not as proud or irascible as Abaddon, nor as ruthless as Sedirae, nor even as solid and venerable as Iacton Qruze, Sejanus was the perfect captain, tempered evenly in all respects. A warrior and a diplomat in equal measure, Sejanus's martial record, second only to Abaddon's, was easily forgotten when in company with the man himself. A beautiful man, Loken would say, building his tale, a beautiful man adored by all. 'No finer figure in Mark IV plate than Hastur Sejanus. That he is remembered, and his deeds celebrated, even here amongst us, speaks of Sejanus's qualities. The noblest hero of the Great Crusade.' That was how Loken would describe him to the eager listeners. 'In future times, he will be recalled with such fondness that men will name their sons after him.'

Sejanus, with a squad of his finest warriors from the Fourth Company, travelled in-system in a gilded barge, and was received for audience by the Emperor at his palace on the third planet.

And killed.

Murdered. Hacked down on the onyx floor of the palace even as he stood before the Emperor's golden throne. Sejanus and his glory squad – Dymos, Malsandar, Gorthoi and the rest – all slaughtered by the Emperor's elite guard, the so-called Invisibles.

Apparently, Sejanus had not offered the correct fealty. Indelicately, he had suggested there might actually be *another* Emperor.

The commander's grief was absolute. He had loved Sejanus like a son. They had warred side by side to affect compliance on a hundred worlds. But the commander, always sanguine and wise in such matters, told his signal men to offer the Emperor another chance. The commander detested resorting to war, and always sought alternative paths away from violence, where such were workable. This was a mistake, he reasoned, a terrible, terrible mistake. Peace could be salvaged. This 'Emperor' could be made to understand.

It was about then, Loken liked to add, that a suggestion of quote marks began to appear around the 'Emperor's' name.

It was determined that a second embassy would be despatched. Maloghurst volunteered at once. The commander agreed, but ordered the speartip forwards into assault range. The intent was clear: one hand extended open, in peace, the other held ready as a fist. If the second embassy failed, or was similarly met with violence, then the fist would already be in position to strike. That sombre day, Loken said, the honour of the speartip had fallen, by the customary drawing of lots, to the strengths of Abaddon, Torgaddon, 'Little Horus' Aximand. And Loken himself.

At the order, battle musters began. The ships of the speartip slipped forward, running under obscurement. On board,

Stormbirds were hauled onto their launch carriages. Weapons were issued and certified. Oaths of moment were sworn and witnessed. Armour was machined into place around the anointed bodies of the chosen.

In silence, tensed and ready to be unleashed, the speartip watched as the shuttle convoy bearing Maloghurst and his envoys arced down towards the third planet. Surface batteries smashed them out of the heavens. As the burning scads of debris from Maloghurst's flotilla billowed away into the atmosphere, the 'Emperor's' fleet elements rose up out of the oceans, out of the high cloud, out of the gravity wells of nearby moons. Six hundred warships, revealed and armed for war.

Abaddon broke obscurement and made a final, personal plea to the 'Emperor', beseeching him to see sense. The warships began to fire on Abaddon's speartip.

'My commander,' Abaddon relayed to the heart of the waiting fleet, 'there is no dealing here. This fool imposter will not listen.'

And the commander replied, 'Illuminate him, my son, but spare all you can. That order not withstanding, avenge the blood of my noble Sejanus. Decimate this "Emperor's" elite murderers, and bring the imposter to me.'

'And so,' Loken would sigh, 'we made war upon our brethren, so lost in ignorance.'

It was late evening, but the sky was saturated with light. The photo-tropic towers of the High City, built to turn and follow the sun with their windows during the day, shifted uneasily at the pulsating radiance in the heavens. Spectral shapes swam high in the upper atmosphere: ships engaging in a swirling mass, charting brief, nonsensical zodiacs with the beams of their battery weapons.

At ground level, around the wide, basalt platforms that formed the skirts of the palace, gunfire streamed through the air like horizontal rain, hosing coils of tracer fire that dipped and slithered heavily like snakes, die-straight zips of energy that vanished as fast as they appeared, and flurries of bolt shells like blizzarding hail. Downed Stormbirds, many of them crippled and burning, littered twenty square kilometres of the landscape.

Black, humanoid figures paced slowly in across the limits of the palace sprawl. They were shaped like armoured men, and they trudged like men, but they were giants, each one hundred and forty metres tall. The Mechanicum had deployed a half-dozen of its Titan war engines. Around the Titans' soot-black ankles, troops flooded forward in a breaking wave three kilometres wide.

The Luna Wolves surged like the surf of the wave, thousands of gleaming white figures bobbing and running forward across the skirt platforms, detonations bursting amongst them, lifting rippling fireballs and trees of dark brown smoke. Each blast juddered the ground with a gritty thump, and showered down dirt as an after-curse. Assault craft swept in over their heads, low, between the shambling frames of the wide-spaced Titans, fanning the slowly lifting smoke clouds into sudden, energetic vortices.

Every Astartes helmet was filled with vox-chatter: snapping voices, chopping back and forth, their tonal edges roughened by the transmission quality.

It was Loken's first taste of mass war since Ullanor. Tenth Company's first taste too. There had been skirmishes and scraps, but nothing testing. Loken was glad to see that his cohort hadn't grown rusty. The unapologetic regimen of live drills and punishing exercises he'd maintained had kept them whetted as sharp and serious as the terms of the oaths of moment they had taken just hours before.

Ullanor had been glorious; a hard, unstinting slog to dislodge and overthrow a bestial empire. The greenskin had been a pernicious and resilient foe, but they had broken his back and kicked over the embers of his revel fires. The commander had won the field through the employment of his favourite, practiced strategy: the speartip thrust to tear out the throat. Ignoring the greenskin masses, which had outnumbered the crusaders five to one, the commander had struck directly at the Overlord and his command coterie, leaving the enemy headless and without direction.

The same philosophy operated here. Tear out the throat and let the body spasm and die. Loken and his men, and the war engines that supported them, were the edge of the blade unsheathed for that purpose.

But this was not like Ullanor at all. No thickets of mud and clay-built ramparts, no ramshackle fortresses of bare metal and wire, no black powder air bursts or howling ogre-foes. This was not a barbaric brawl determined by blades and upper body strength.

This was modern warfare in a civilised place. This was man against man, inside the monolithic precincts of a cultured people. The enemy possessed ordnance and firearms every bit the technological match of the Legion forces, and the skill and training to use them. Through the green imaging of his visor, Loken saw armoured men with energy weapons ranged against them in the lower courses of the palace. He saw tracked weapon carriages, automated artillery; nests of four or even eight automatic cannons shackled together on cart platforms that lumbered forward on hydraulic legs.

Not like Ullanor at all. That had been an ordeal. This would be a test. Equal against equal. Like against like.

Except that for all its martial technologies, the enemy lacked one essential quality, and that quality was locked within each and every case of Mark IV power armour: the genetically enhanced flesh and blood of the Imperial Astartes. Modified, refined, post-human, the Astartes were superior to anything they had met or would ever meet. No fighting force in the galaxy could ever hope to match the Legions, unless the stars went out, and madness ruled, and lawful sense turned upside down. For, as Sedirae had once said, 'The only thing that can beat an Astartes is another Astartes', and they had all laughed at that. The impossible was nothing to be scared of.

The enemy – their armour a polished magenta trimmed in silver, as Loken later discovered when he viewed them with his helmet off – firmly held the induction gates into the inner palace. They were big men, tall, thick through the chest and shoulders, and at the peak of fitness. Not one of them, not even the tallest, came up to the chin of one of the Luna Wolves. It was like fighting children.

Well-armed children, it had to be said.

Through the billowing smoke and the jarring detonations, Loken led the veteran First Squad up the steps at a run, the plasteel soles of their boots grating on the stone: First Squad, Tenth Company, Hellebore Tactical Squad, gleaming giants in pearl-white armour, the wolf head insignia stark black on their auto-responsive shoulder plates. Crossfire zigzagged around them from the defended gates ahead. The night air shimmered with the heat distortion of weapons discharge. Some kind of upright, automated mortar was casting a sluggish, flaccid stream of fat munition charges over their heads.

'Kill it!' Loken heard Brother-Sergeant Jubal instruct over

the link. Jubal's order was given in the curt argot of Ctho-
nia, their derivation world, a language that the Luna Wolves
had preserved as their battle-tongue.

The battle-brother carrying the squad's plasma cannon
obeyed without hesitation. For a dazzling half-second, a
twenty-metre ribbon of light linked the muzzle of his weapon
to the auto-mortar, and then the device engulfed the facade
of the palace in a roasting wash of yellow flame.

Dozens of enemy soldiers were cast down by the blast.
Several were thrown up into the air, landing crumpled and
boneless on the flight of steps.

'Into them!' Jubal barked.

Wildfire chipped and pattered off their armour. Loken felt
the distant sting of it. Brother Calends stumbled and fell, but
righted himself again, almost at once.

Loken saw the enemy scatter away from their charge. He
swung his bolter up. His weapon had a gash in the metal of
the foregrip, the legacy of a greenskin's axe during Ullanor,
a cosmetic mark Loken had told the armourers not to finish out. He began to fire, not on burst, but on single shot,
feeling the weapon buck and kick against his palms. Bolter
rounds were explosive penetrators. The men he hit popped
like blisters, or shredded like bursting fruit. Pink mist fumed
off every ruptured figure as it fell.

'Tenth Company!' Loken shouted. 'For the Warmaster!'

The war cry was still unfamiliar, just another aspect of the
newness. It was the first time Loken had declaimed it in war,
the first chance he'd had since the honour had been bestowed
by the Emperor after Ullanor.

By the Emperor. The true Emperor.

'Lupercal! Lupercal!' the Wolves yelled back as they streamed
in, choosing to answer with the old cry, the Legion's pet-

name for their beloved commander. The warhorns of the Titans boomed.

They stormed the palace. Loken paused by one of the induction gates, urging his front-runners in, carefully reviewing the advance of his company main force. Hellish fire continued to rake them from the upper balconies and towers. In the far distance, a brilliant dome of light suddenly lifted into the sky, astonishingly bright and vivid. Loken's visor automatically dimmed. The ground trembled and a noise like a thunderclap reached him. A capital ship of some size, stricken and ablaze, had fallen out of the sky and impacted in the outskirts of the High City. Drawn by the flash, the phototropic towers above him fidgeted and rotated.

Reports flooded in. Aximand's force, Fifth Company, had secured the Regency and the pavilions on the ornamental lakes to the west of the High City. Torgaddon's men were driving up through the lower town, slaying the armour sent to block them.

Loken looked east. Three kilometres away, across the flat plain of the basalt platforms, across the tide of charging men and striding Titans and stitching fire, Abaddon's company, First Company, was crossing the bulwarks into the far flank of the palace. Loken magnified his view, resolving hundreds of white-armoured figures pouring through the smoke and chop-fire. At the front of them, the dark figures of First Company's foremost Terminator squad, the Justaerin. They wore polished black armour, dark as night, as if they belonged to some other, black Legion.

'Loken to First,' he sent. 'Tenth has entry.'

There was a pause, a brief distort, then Abaddon's voice answered. 'Loken, Loken... are you trying to shame me with your diligence?'

'Not for a moment, First Captain,' Loken replied. There was a strict hierarchy of respect within the Legion, and though he was a senior officer, Loken regarded the peerless First Captain with awe. All of the Mournival, in fact, though Torgaddon had always favoured Loken with genuine shows of friendship.

Now Sejanus was gone, Loken thought. The aspect of the Mournival would soon change.

'I'm playing with you, Loken,' Abaddon sent, his voice so deep that some vowel sounds were blurred by the vox. 'I'll meet you at the feet of this false Emperor. First one there gets to illuminate him.'

Loken fought back a smile. Ezekyle Abaddon had seldom sported with him before. He felt blessed, elevated. To be a chosen man was enough, but to be in with the favoured elite, that was every captain's dream.

Reloading, Loken entered the palace through the induction gate, stepping over the tangled corpses of the enemy dead. The plaster facings of the inner walls had been cracked and blown down, and loose crumbs, like dry sand, crunched under his feet. The air was full of smoke, and his visor display kept jumping from one register to another as it attempted to compensate and get a clean reading.

He moved down the inner hall, hearing the echo of gunfire from deeper in the palace compound. The body of a brother lay slumped in a doorway to his left, the large, white-armoured corpse odd and out of place amongst the smaller enemy bodies. Marjex, one of the Legion's Apothecaries, was bending over him. He glanced up as Loken approached, and shook his head.

'Who is it?' Loken asked.

'Tibor, of Second Squad,' Marjex replied. Loken frowned as he saw the devastating head wound that had stopped Tibor.

'The Emperor knows his name,' Loken said.

Marjex nodded, and reached into his narthecium to get the reductor tool. He was about to remove Tibor's precious gene-seed, so that it might be returned to the Legion banks.

Loken left the Apothecary to his work, and pushed on down the hall. In a wide colonnade ahead, the towering walls were decorated with frescoes, showing familiar scenes of a haloed Emperor upon a golden throne. How blind these people are, Loken thought, how sad this is. One day, one single day with the iterators, and they would understand. We are not the enemy. We are the same, and we bring with us a glorious message of redemption. Old Night is done. Man walks the stars again, and the might of the Astartes walks at his side to keep him safe.

In a broad, sloping tunnel of etched silver, Loken caught up with elements of Third Squad. Of all the units in his company, Third Squad – Locasta Tactical Squad – was his favourite and his favoured. Its commander, Brother-Sergeant Nero Vipus, was his oldest and truest friend.

'How's your humour, captain?' Vipus asked. His pearl-white plate was smudged with soot and streaked with blood.

'Phlegmatic, Nero. You?'

'Choleric. Red-raged, in fact. I've just lost a man, and two more of mine are injured. There's something covering the junction ahead. Something heavy. Rate of fire like you wouldn't believe.'

'Tried fragging it?'

'Two or three grenades. No effect. And there's nothing to see. Garvi, we've all heard about these so-called Invisibles. The ones that butchered Sejanus. I was wondering–'

'Leave the wondering to me,' Loken said. 'Who's down?'

Vipus shrugged. He was a little taller than Loken, and his

shrug made the heavy ribbing and plates of his armour clunk together. 'Zakias.'

'Zakias? No...'

'Torn into shreds before my very eyes. Oh, I feel the hand of the ship on me, Garvi.'

The hand of the ship. An old saying. The commander's flagship was called the *Vengeful Spirit*, and in times of duress or loss, the Wolves liked to draw upon all that implied as a charm, a totem of retribution.

'In Zakias's name,' Vipus growled, 'I'll find this bastard Invisible and–'

'Sooth your choler, brother. I've no use for it,' Loken said. 'See to your wounded while I take a look.'

Vipus nodded and redirected his men. Loken pushed up past them to the disputed junction.

It was a vault-roofed crossways where four hallways met. The area read cold and still to his imaging. Fading smoke wisped up into the rafters. The ouslite floor had been chewed and peppered with thousands of impact craters. Brother Zakias, his body as yet unretrieved, lay in pieces at the centre of the crossway, a steaming pile of shattered white plasteel and bloody meat.

Vipus had been right. There was no sign of an enemy present. No heat-trace, not even a flicker of movement. But studying the area, Loken saw a heap of empty shell cases, glittering brass, that had spilled out from behind a bulkhead across from him. Was that where the killer was hiding?

Loken bent down and picked up a chunk of fallen plasterwork. He lobbed it into the open. There was a click, and then a hammering deluge of autofire raked across the junction. It lasted five seconds, and in that time over a thousand rounds were expended. Loken saw the fuming shell cases spitting out from behind the bulkhead as they were ejected.

The firing stopped. Fycelene vapour fogged the junction. The gunfire had scored a mottled gouge across the stone floor, pummelling Zakias's corpse in the process. Spots of blood and scraps of tissue had been spattered out.

Loken waited. He heard a whine and the metallic clunk of an autoloader system. He read weapon heat, fading, but no body warmth.

'Won a medal yet?' Vipus asked, approaching.

'It's just an automatic sentry gun,' Loken replied.

'Well, that's a small relief at least,' Vipus said. 'After the grenades we've pitched in that direction, I was beginning to wonder if these vaunted Invisibles might be "Invulnerables" too. I'll call up Devastator support to-'

'Just give me a light flare,' Loken said.

Vipus stripped one off his leg plate and handed it to his captain. Loken ignited it with a twist of his hand, and threw it down the hallway opposite. It bounced, fizzling, glaring white hot, past the hidden killer.

There was a grind of servos. The implacable gunfire began to roar down the corridor at the flare, kicking it and bouncing it, ripping into the floor.

'Garvi-' Vipus began.

Loken was running. He crossed the junction, thumped his back against the bulkhead. The gun was still blazing. He wheeled round the bulkhead and saw the sentry gun, built into an alcove. A squat machine, set on four pad feet and heavily plated, it had turned its short, fat, pumping cannons away from him to fire on the distant, flickering flare.

Loken reached over and tore out a handful of its servo flexes. The guns stuttered and died.

'We're clear!' Loken called out. Locasta moved up.

'That's generally called showing off,' Vipus remarked.

Loken led Locasta up the corridor, and they entered a fine state apartment. Other apartment chambers, similarly regal, beckoned beyond. It was oddly still and quiet.

'Which way now?' Vipus asked.

'We go find this "Emperor",' Loken said.

Vipus snorted. 'Just like that?'

'The First Captain bet me I couldn't reach him first.'

'The First Captain, eh? Since when was Garviel Loken on pally terms with him?'

'Since Tenth breached the palace ahead of First. Don't worry, Nero, I'll remember you little people when I'm famous.'

Nero Vipus laughed, the sound snuffling out of his helmet mask like the cough of a consumptive bull.

What happened next didn't make either of them laugh at all.

YOUR
NEXT READ

HORUS RISING
by Dan Abnett

After thousands of years of expansion and conquest, the human Imperium is at its height. His dream for humanity accomplished, the Emperor hands over the reins of power to his Warmaster, Horus, and heads back to Terra.

SOUL WARS

JOSH REYNOLDS

CHAPTER ONE

BLACK PYRAMID

NAGASHIZZAR, THE SILENT CITY

At the heart of the Realm of Death, the Undying King waited on his basalt throne.

He sat in silence, counting the moments with a patience that had worn down mountains and dried out seas. Spiders wove their webs across his eyes, and worms burrowed in his bones, but he paid them no mind. Such little lives were beneath the notice of Nagash. His awareness was elsewhere, bent towards the Great Work.

Then, Nagash stiffened, alert. Purple light flared deep in the black sockets of his eyes. The scattered facets of his perceptions contracted. The disparate realms slid away, as all his attentions focused on Shyish and the lands he claimed for his own.

Something was wrong. A flaw in the formulas. Something unforeseen. The air pulsed with raw, primal life. It beat upon the edges of his perceptions like a hot wind. He shrank down further still, peering through the eyes of his servants – the skeletal guardians that patrolled the streets endlessly. He saw… green. Not the green of vegetation, but dark green, the solid green musculature of things that should not be in Nagashizzar. He heard the thunder of rawhide drums and tasted a hot, animal stink on the air.

Something was amiss. *Inconceivable*. And yet it was happening.

Nagash shook off the dust of centuries and forced himself to his feet. The creaking of his bones was like the toppling of trees. Bats and spirits spun in a shrieking typhoon about him as he strode from his silent throne room, shaking the chamber with every step. He was trailed, as ever, by nine heavy tomes, chained to his form. The flabby, fleshy covers of the grimoires writhed and snapped like wild beasts at nearby spirits.

He cast open the great black iron doors, startling those of his servants in the pillared forecourt beyond. That the flesh-less lords of his deathrattle legions were gathered here before the doors of his throne room, rather than seeing to their duties, only stoked the fires of his growing anger. 'Arkhan,' he rasped, in a voice like a tomb-wind. 'Attend me.'

'I am here, my king.'

Arkhan the Black, Mortarch of Sacrament and vizier to the Undying King, stepped forwards, surrounded by a gaggle of lesser liches. The wizened, long-dead sorcerers huddled in Arkhan's shadow, as if seeking protection from the god they had served briefly in life and now forever in death. Unlike his subordinates, Arkhan was no withered husk, for all that he lacked any flesh on his dark bones. Clad in robes of rich purple and gold, and wearing war-plate of the same hue, he radiated a power second only to that of his master.

Nagash knew this to be so, for he had made a gift of that power, in days long gone by. Arkhan was the Hand of Death and the castellan of Nagashizzar. He was the vessel through which the will of Nagash was enacted. He had no purpose, save that which Nagash gifted him. 'Speak, my servant. What transpires at the edges of my awareness?'

'Best you see for yourself, my lord. Words cannot do it justice.'

Though Arkhan lacked any expression except a black-toothed rictus, Nagash thought his servant was amused. Arkhan turned and swept out his staff of office, scattering liches and spirits from their path as he led his master to one of the massive balconies that clustered along the tower's length. At his gesture, deathrattle guards, clad in the pano-ply of long-extinct kingdoms, fell into a protective formation around Nagash. While the Undying King had no particu-lar fear of assassins, he was content to indulge Arkhan's paranoia.

'We appear to have an infestation of vermin, my lord,' Arkhan said, as they stepped onto the balcony. 'Quite persis-tent vermin, in fact.' Razarak, Arkhan's dread abyssal mount, lay sprawled upon the stones, feasting on a keening spirit. The beast, made from bone and black iron, its body a cage for the skulls of traitors and cowards, gave an interrogative grunt as its master strode past. It fell silent as it caught sight of Nagash, and returned to its repast.

Many-pillared Nagashizzar, the Silent City, spread out before him. It was a thing of cold, beautiful calculus, laid out according to the ancient formulas of the Corpse Geometries. A machine of stone and shadow, intricate in its solidity, com-fortable in its predictability.

It was a place of lightless avenues of black stone veined

with purple, and empty squares, where dark structures rose in grim reverence to his will. These cyclopean monuments were made from bricks of shadeglass, the vitrified form of the collected grave-sands. Harder than steel and polished smooth, the towering edifices resonated with the winds of death.

Nagashizzar had been made from the first mountain to rise from the eternal seas. There had been another city like it, once, in another time, in another world, and Nagash had ruled it as well. Now all that was left of that grand kingdom were threadbare memories, which fluttered like moths at the edges of his consciousness.

Those memories had taken root here and grown into a silent memorial. Or perhaps a mockery. Even Nagash did not know which it was. Regardless, Nagashizzar was his, as it had always been and always would be. Such was the constancy of his vision.

But now, that vision was being tested.

Nagash detected a familiar scent. The air throbbed with the beat of savage drums and bellowing cries. Muscular, simian shapes, clad in ill-fitting and crudely wrought armour, loped through the dusty streets of Nagashizzar. Orruks. The bestial, primitive children of Gorkamorka.

Below, phalanxes of skeletal warriors assembled in the plazas and wide avenues, seeking to stem the green tide, but to no avail. The orruks shook the ground with the joyful fury of their charge. A roaring Maw-krusha slammed through a pillar, sending chunks of stone hurtling across the plaza. It trampled the dead as it loped through their ranks, and the orruk crouched on its back whooped in satisfaction.

The orruks were the antithesis of the disciplined armies facing them. For them, warfare and play were one and the same, and they approached both with brutal gusto. They brawled with the dead, bellowing nonsensical challenges to the unheeding tomb-legions. There was no objective here, save destruction. Unless…

Nagash turned towards the centre of the city, where the flat expanse of the Black Pyramid towered over the skyline. It was the greatest and grandest of the monuments he'd ordered constructed. Unlike its smaller kin, hundreds of which dotted Shyish, the Black Pyramid was the fulcrum of his efforts. Its apex stretched down into Nekroheim, the underworld below Nagashizzar, while its base sprawled across the city – a colossal structure built upside down at Shyish's heart.

A flicker of unease passed through him as he considered the implications of the sudden assault. It was not a coincidence. It could not be. He looked at Arkhan. 'Where did they come from?'

The Mortarch motioned southwards with his staff. 'Through the Jackal's Eye,' he said. Nagash's gaze sharpened as he followed Arkhan's gesture. The Jackal's Eye was a realmgate, leading to the Ghurish Hinterlands. There were many such dimensional apertures scattered across this region – pathways between Shyish and the other Mortal Realms. They were guarded at all times by his most trusted warriors. Or so he had commanded, a century or more ago. As if privy to his master's thoughts, Arkhan said, 'Whoever let them pass through will be punished, my lord. I will see to it personally.'

'If the orruks are here, then whoever was guarding the gate is no more. The reasons for their failure are of no interest to me.' Nagash considered the problem before him. Then, as was his right as god and king, he passed it to another, one whose entire purpose was to deal with such trivialities.

'Arkhan, see to the disposal of these creatures.' Nagash looked down at his Mortarch. Arkhan met his gaze without flinching. Fear, along with almost everything else, had been burned out of the liche in his millennia of servitude. 'I go to bring the Great Work to its conclusion, before it is undone by this interruption.'

'As you command, my lord.' Arkhan struck the black stones of the balcony with the ferrule of his staff. Razarak heaved itself to its feet with a rustling hiss. The dread abyssal stalked forwards, and Arkhan hauled himself smoothly into the saddle. He caught up the reins and glanced at Nagash. 'I am your servant. As ever.'

Nagash detected something that might have been disdain in Arkhan's flat tones. Of course, such was impossible. The Mortarch was no more capable of defying Nagash than the skeletons trudging through the wastes. And yet, he seemed to, in innumerable small ways. As if there were a flaw in him – or in Nagash himself.

For a moment, the facets of Nagash's being hesitated. Then, as ever, the black machinery that passed for his soul righted itself and continued on. He had been mistaken. There was no defiance. Only loyalty. All were one, in Nagash, and Nagash was all. 'Go,' he said, the stentorian echo of his command causing the air itself to shudder and crack.

With a sharp cry, the Mortarch urged his steed into a loping run. The skeletal monstrosity galloped across the balcony and flung itself into the air. The winds of death wrapped protectively about both rider and steed, carrying them towards the battle.

A moment later, a cyclone of howling, tortured spirits streamed past Nagash and spiralled into the air in pursuit of the Mortarch. He watched as they hurtled upwards and away, a cacophonous fog of murderous spectres, twisted and broken by his will into a shape suited to their task. They had been criminals, murderers and traitors in life, and now, in death, they were bound in stocks and chains, afflicted with terrible hungers that could never be sated. Nagash knew himself to be a just god, whatever else.

He turned away, satisfied. Arkhan would see it done, or be destroyed in the attempt. The Mortarch had been destroyed before and would be again. Always, Nagash resurrected him. His term of service had no end, for so long as the Undying King required his services.

He cast his gaze back towards the Black Pyramid and let his body crumble to dust and bone. Even as it came apart, his mind was racing through the confines of the pyramid like an ill wind. Its interior was a labyrinth of impeccably placed tunnels and passageways, all polished to a mirror-sheen. These pathways resonated with the energies of the aetheric void that encompassed and permeated the Mortal Realms, invisible and inescapable.

Construction had begun in the depths below Nagashizzar, in the underworld of Nekroheim, the wells from which all other underworlds had sprung. The dead of entire civilisations had surrendered their bones to form the walls and ceiling of the cavernous reaches of the underworld. The vast expanse was lit by a dead sun, the flickering wraith of an ancient orb long since snuffed, stretched upwards from the deepest pit in the underworld. Its sickly radiance cast shrouds of frost and fog wherever it stretched, and an eternal corona of wailing souls orbited it.

Now, that sun churned malignantly, its incandescent heart pierced by a capstone crafted from purest grave-sand. He had placed that capstone himself, with his own hands. Only through his magics, and the fluid nature of Nekroheim, had such a feat of engineering been possible. The Black Pyramid had blossomed from that point, spreading outwards and upwards with glacial certainty.

Once, the black pyramids had been the wellsprings of his power, designed to draw in the souls of the dead, like fish in a net. Most were gone now, reduced to rubble by the rampaging armies of the Ruinous Powers.

But this one eclipsed them all, in both size and purpose. Every element of its construction was bent towards drawing the raw stuff of magic itself, from the edges of Shyish, to its heart. The greatest concentration of those magics which sustained the Realm of Death would be refracted and reflected through the pyramid. Thus would the raw magics be refined into a more useful form. It had been constructed over the course of aeons, assembled by generations of artisans, both alive and dead. And now, it was complete, awaiting only his presence to fulfil its function.

His spirit raced through the passageways, and where he passed, the skeletal servitors scattered throughout them twitched into motion, following their master into the hollow heart of the pyramid. This central chamber spread outwards from the structure's core, from capstone to base, banded by pillared tiers, one for each level of the pyramid.

As Nagash's spirit billowed into the immense chamber like a black cloud, silent overseers, stationed among the pillars, stirred for the first time in centuries. They directed the new arrivals onto the assemblage of walkways and ledges that extended from the tiers towards the hundreds of platforms that clung to the central core of the pyramid.

The core stood in stark contrast to the orderly nature of the rest of the structure. It was a contorted spine of jagged shadeglass, reaching from the interior of the capstone up to a glittering field of amethyst stalactites that spread across the pyramid's base. A web of shimmering strands stretched out from the core in quaquaversal spillage. The core and its calcified web were covered in innumerable facets of varying sizes and shapes, all of which shone with a malevolent energy.

To Nagash, that light was almost blinding. It throbbed with morbid potential, and he felt the Black Pyramid's monstrous hunger almost as keenly as his own. It clawed greedily at his essence, but he resisted its pull with an ease born of long exposure. It feasted on the strength of the realm, battening on the winds of death, as he would feast on it, in his turn.

His deathrattle slaves entered the chamber, and many of the skeletal labourers were ripped from their feet and drawn into a sudden crackling storm of amethyst energies, as Nagash drew their essences into his own. With brisk efficiency, he disassembled the unliving slaves and reassembled them into a new body for himself.

The God of Death flexed a newly fashioned hand, feeling the weight of new bones. Satisfied, he stepped onto the largest of the walkways. Ancient warriors, clad in rusty, age-blackened armour, knelt as he passed through their ranks. Deathrattle champions and lords, the kings and queens of a hundred fleshless fiefdoms, humbled themselves before the one they acknowledged as their god and emperor both. The diminished husks of slaves and artisans abased themselves, grovelling before the master of their destinies. Nagash surveyed the silent ranks and was pleased.

At the urging of the overseers, skeletons trooped across the walkways to the great platforms clinging to the core. Occupying each platform was a millstone-like ring of shade-glass, dotted with turning spokes of bone. These lined the core's length, from top to bottom, one atop the next, rising upwards along the spine. Strange sigils marked the crudely carved circumference of each ring, and these glowed with a pallid radiance.

'The time has come,' Nagash said, as the last of the skeletons assumed its position. The walls of the shaft hummed in time to his words. As one, his servants stiffened, their witch-light gazes fixed upon him. 'Go to your prepared places, and bend yourself against the wheel of progress. Let it turn and time itself be ground between the stones of my will.'

The fleshless shoulders of princes and slaves alike bent to the spokes of each wheel. As the skeletons pushed against the spokes, the stone rings began to move. A thunderous, grinding growl filled the air. Violet lightning flashed across the facets of the web and sprang outwards, striking the polished walls of the shaft.

A rumble began, far below. It shuddered upwards through the pyramid, shaking it to its upside-down foundations. Loose grave-sand sifted down like dry rain. Nagash, still standing atop the largest walkway, stretched out a talon, gathering together the strands of crackling energy that seared the air. With precise, calculated movements, he looped the shimmering skeins of magic about his forearms, as if they were chains. The skeins flared, burning as he pulled them taut, but he ignored the pain. After all, what was pain to a god?

Facing the core, Nagash gathered more and more of the skeins, and his titanic form became a conductor. Amethyst lightning crawled across him, winnowing into the hollow places and filling him with strength enough to crack the vaults of the heavens. This was not the raw magic that soured the edges of his realm, but a purified form.

He hauled back on the strands of magic he held, lending his strength to that of his servants. As they pushed, he pulled, forcing the great machinery into motion. Around him, the faceted walls began to shift and scrape as slowly, surely, the Black Pyramid began to revolve on its capstone, as he had designed it to do.

The structure rotated faster and faster. The dead sun beneath it flared brightly, as if in panic, and then burst with a cataclysmic scream that shook Nekroheim to its intangible roots. Rivers of cold fire streaked up the sides of the pyramid, flowing towards the base, or else washed across the cavern walls. Nekroheim itself shuddered, as if wounded.

The cavern floor began to churn and shift. Millions of bones clattered as the rotation of the pyramid drew them in its wake. Like some vast, calcified whirlpool, the entirety of the underworld was soon in motion. A storm of bones and tattered spirits, spinning about the ever-turning pyramid.

Within the pyramid's heart, Nagash felt and saw all of this in the polished walls of shadeglass. He saw the streaks of purple light stretching out, flowering into storms of raging elemental fire as they broke through the borders that separated Nekroheim from the other underworlds. The purple light dug into the metaphysical substance of these other realms, hooking them the way a meat-hook might sink into a side of beef. Steadily, they were drawn towards Nekroheim, becoming part of the growing maelstrom.

Nagash threw back his head and bellowed. He felt as if he was on the cusp of dissolution, as if the monstrous energies he sought to manipulate now threatened to rip him asunder. Only his will prevented him from succumbing to the forces he'd unleashed. A lesser god would have dissolved into howling oblivion. He clawed at the storm of magic, drawing more of it into himself, pulling the world-spanning chains tight.

Outside the pyramid, Nekroheim was crumbling. Changing

shape. The underworld bent beneath the oscillating structure, bowing up around it. Becoming something new.

The reverberations rippled outwards across Shyish. Through the eyes of his servants, Nagash saw the skies above Nagashiz-zar turn purple-black. Orruks wailed as their green flesh sloughed from their bones, and they collapsed in on them-selves. Billions of skull-faced beetles poured down from the swirling clouds, devouring those greenskins that were still in one piece. Nagash laughed, low, loud and long as the ground beneath Nagashizzar began to buckle and sink. Soon, every realm would feel the echoes of what he did here. Reality would shape itself to accommodate his will.

His laughter ceased as shadeglass cracked and splintered all around him. Something moved within the polished depths. They came slowly, drifting through the dark: vast impressions with no definable shape or form. The air of the chamber stank of hot iron and spoiled blood, of sour meat and strange incenses. He heard the rasp of sharp-edged feathers and the clank of great chains. He felt the flutter of unseen flies, clus-tering about his skull, and their hum filled the hollows of his form.

Something that might have been a face slipped across the cracked facets. It gibbered soundlessly, but Nagash heard its words nonetheless. It spoke in a voice that only gods could discern, spewing curses. He turned as something that might have been a blade, wreathed in fire, struck another facet. More cracks shivered outwards from the point of impact. Nagash did not flinch. To his left, enormous talons, as of some great bird, scratched at the shadeglass, while opposite them, a flabby paw-shape, filthy and sore-ridden, left streaks of bubbling excrescence along the facets.

Eyes like dying stars fixed him with a glare, and a howl

shook Nekroheim to its roots. Great fangs, made from thousands of splintered swords and molten rock, gnashed in elemental fury. Nagash lifted a hand in mocking greeting. 'Hail, old horrors – I see that I have your attention.'

The Ruinous Powers had come like sharks, stirred from the deep places by a storm, as he'd known they would. They came roaring, thrusting the barest edges of their inhuman perceptions into his realm. Was it curiosity that had drawn them so – or fear?

He felt their awareness as a sudden pressure upon him, as if a great weight had fallen on him from all angles. The immensities circled him through the facets of the walls, prowling like beasts held at bay by firelight. 'But you are too late. It is begun.'

Something bellowed, and great claws of brass and fire pressed against the reverse of the shadeglass, cracking it. An avian shadow peered down through the facets of the ceiling, whispering in many voices. The stink of rot and putrification choked the air. Had any of his servants been alive, they might have suffocated from the stench. Voices like the groaning of the earth or the death-screams of stars cursed him and demanded he cease.

He cast his defiance into their teeth. 'Who are you to demand anything of me? I am Nagash. I am eternal. I have walked in the deep places for long enough and have gathered my strength. I will shatter mountains and dry the seas.'

He turned as they circled him, keeping them in sight. 'I shall pull down the sun and cast the earth into the sky. All of time will be set aflame and all impurities in the blood of existence burnt away, by my will and mine alone. There shall be no gods before me, and none after.' He gestured sharply. 'All will be Nagash. Nagash will be all.'

As the echo of his words faded, something laughed. A ghost of a sound, no more substantial than the wind. Nagash paused. Something was wrong. Belatedly, he realised that the Ruinous Powers would not have come, unless there was some amusement to be had. Not the orruks, but something else. Some other flaw in his design.

'What mischief have you wrought?' he intoned. He found it a moment later. Familiar soul-scents, bitter and tarry, wafted on the currents of power flowing through the edifice. Tiny souls, these. Like bits of broken glass. The skaven spoke in hissing, squealing tones as they scuttled through the pyramid, wrapped in cloaks of purest shadow. He did not know by what magics the ratkin had avoided the guardians of this place. Nor did he care. That they were here, now, was the only important thing.

It seemed the orruks were not the only ones who had come seeking the treasures of Nagashizzar. He looked up, into the insubstantial faces of his foes. 'Is this, then, the best you can do? You send vermin to stop me?' The laughter of the Dark Gods continued, growing in volume. Incensed, a part of his consciousness sheared off and slipped into the depths of the pyramid, seeking the origin of the disturbance while the rest of him concentrated on completing the ritual he'd begun.

His penumbral facet swept through the passages and pathways like a cold wind, but moving far more swiftly than any natural gust. He found them in the labyrinthine depths, chipping away at the very foundation stones of the pyramid. Their desire for the vitrified magics was palpable. The skaven had ever been a greedy race.

How long had they been here, pilfering the fruits of his labours? How had they gone unnoticed, until now? As their tools scraped at the bricks of shadeglass, crackles of purple lightning flowed through the walls. The more they collected, the greater the destabilisation became. Nagash watched the arcs of lightning, tracing their routes and calculating the destruction they would wreak.

Somewhere, at the bottom of the deep well of his memories, something stirred, and he had the vaguest impression that all of this had happened before. The pyramid, his triumph, the skaven, it all felt suddenly – awfully – familiar. God though he was, he could not well recall his existence before Sigmar had freed him, though he knew that he had existed. He had always existed. But he could recall only a few scattered moments, frozen in his recollections like insects in amber – instances of pain and frustration, of triumph and treachery. Was that what this was? Had he lived through this moment – or something like it – before? Was that why the dark gods laughed so? He paused, considering. The black clockwork of his mind calculating.

The Mortal Realms were something new, built on the bones of the old. They were merely the latest iteration of the universal cycle and would one day shatter and reform, as had countless realities before them. As sure as the scythe reaped the grain, all things ended. Nagash knew this and understood, for he was death, and death was the only constant. But what if there had been a time that he had not been as he was?

And what if that time might come again?

What if this was the first step towards that unthinkable moment? And what if he had walked this path before, always with the same beginning and same ending?

Driven by this thought, Nagash let his essence fill the corridor like a graveyard mist, though his body remained in the core, wracked by amethyst lightning. He felt a bite of pain as the rite continued, and he rose up over the ratkin, crackling with wrath. He crushed the closest, snaring it in a foggy talon.

At its demise, he pushed all doubt aside. If this moment had happened before, so be it. The outcome would change. Must change. He would hold fast to his course, whatever the consequences. He would not – could not – be denied. Time itself would buckle before him.

Skaven squealed and scuttled away, fleeing the damp coils of fog. The slowest perished first, bits of shadeglass clatter-ing to the floor as they convulsed and died. The mist filled their contorted forms, dragging them upright and sending them in pursuit of their fellows. The dead ratkin clawed at those they caught, ripping gobbets of fur and meat from their cringing forms. The skaven descended into an orgy of vio-lence, hacking and stabbing at one another in their panic, unable to tell friend from foe.

If this was the first step, he had taken it, and there was nothing to be done. If not, then he still had a chance to see his design through. As the last of the intruders perished, in fear and madness, Nagash dismissed them from his thoughts. Their remains would join the rest of his chattel. There were more important matters to attend to now.

The presence of the intruders had thrown off the delicate balance of the pyramid's function. He could feel it, in the curdled marrow of his bones. They had polluted it some-how, tainted his Great Work. That had been their purpose all along. He could see it now – an antithetical formula, let loose among the Corpse Geometries, to gnaw at the roots of his perfect order. An artificial miscalculation, meant to break him.

Always, they sought to despoil the order he brought. Always, they made sport of his determination. They sent their servants

to cast down his temples, and inflicted a hundred indigni-
ties upon his person. Again and again, they drove him to
the earth, chaining him in one grave after another. They set
stones upon him and sought to bury him where he might be
forgotten forevermore. The laughter of the Ruinous Powers
shook the pyramid, and shadeglass fissured all about him.

They thought him beaten. They thought that once more
he would be cast down into a cairn of their making, to be
safely ignored until the next turn of the wheel. Anger pulsed
through him, and amethyst light flared from the cracks in
his bones.

He was not beaten. And he would never be buried again.

'Stand not between the Undying King and his chosen
course, little gods,' Nagash said. 'Nagash is death, and death
cannot be defeated.' As he spoke, his thoughts raced through
the structure, seeking a way to compensate for the damage.
He was too close to fail now. There must be a way. There *was*
a way. He merely had to divine it.

Skeletons were caught up in a grave-wind, disassembled
and reconstructed as Nagash took shape at the points of
greatest stress – many Undying Kings rose up, a hundred
eyes and a hundred hands, driven by one will. These aspects
of him set their shoulders against collapsing archways, or
braced sagging walls. 'I will not be undone. Not again.' The
words echoed from the mouths of each of his selves, as they
fought against the pyramid's dissolution. A chorus of denials.

Shadeglass cracked and splintered as the oscillation sped
up. Blocks of vitrified sand shifted and split, sliding from
position to crash down around him. But still, the Black
Pyramid revolved. Nagash reached out with mind and form,
seeking to hold the edifice together through sheer determination. Despite his efforts, sections peeled away and

crumbled to dust. Passages collapsed, pulverising thousands of servitors.

The core twisted as if in pain. Cracks raced along its length, leaking tarry magic. The mechanisms of rotation ruptured and burst, hurled aside by the core's convulsions. Skeletons were dashed against the walls, or sent tumbling into the depths of the pyramid. Nagash ignored all of this, focused on containing the magics that now surged all but unchecked and unfiltered through the structure. The power burned through him, threatening to consume him. But he held tight to it. His Great Work would not be undone. Not like this.

'I will not be defeated by vermin. I will not be humbled by lesser gods. I am Nagash. I am supreme.' His denial boomed out, echoing through the pyramid. Through the eyes of innumerable servants, he saw Shyish fold and bend like a burial shroud caught in a cold wind. Wild magic raced outwards, across the amethyst sands.

Across the realms, a rain of black light wept down from the convulsing sky. A million forgotten graves burst open. In vaulted tombs, the honoured dead awoke. Spirits stirred in shadowed bowers and hidden places. Nagash roared wordlessly and drew the power to him, refusing to let it escape. It was his. And he would not let it go. Let the realms crack asunder, let the stars burn out, let silence reign. Nagash would endure.

He could feel the realm buckling around him, changing shape, even as the dark gods laughed mockingly. Reality itself shook, like a tree caught in a hurricane wind.

Until, all at once, their laughter ceased.

And in the long silence that followed... Death smiled.

YOUR
NEXT READ

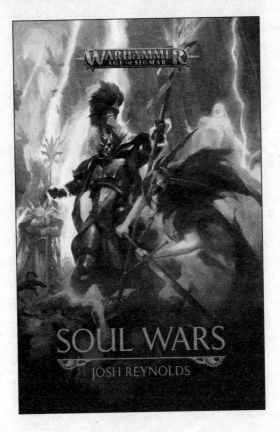

SOUL WARS
by Josh Reynolds

Nagash is rising. As his legions march forth from Shyish to bring death to all the realms, the Anvils of the Heldenhammer stand firm in Glymmsforge, a city of Order in the heart of Nagash's domain…

SACROSANCT

C L WERNER

CHAPTER ONE

Thunder rolled above the vast forest, shaking needles from the ancient pines. Birds took wing, screeching in fright as they rose into the clouds. They wheeled away from the great stream of lightning that crackled through the air. With the storm to spawn it, a bolt struck earthwards and crashed amongst the trees with a deafening roar. A great pillar of smoke and dust was thrown into the sky, rocks and splinters pelting the ground miles from where the lightning struck.

A vast swathe had been gouged from the forest, the ground blackened and the trees knocked flat for a hundred yards in every direction, as though a titan's paw had pressed down upon them. Thick and dark with earth, the pall caused by the impact billowed outwards, throwing a gritty fog across the woods.

Figures moved in that fog, striding from the very midst of the devastation. In such daylight as pierced the smoke, they became more than indistinct shadows. Hulking men clad in armour of gold and blue. Their countenances were hidden behind crested helms with glowering masks. Upon their shields they bore an emblem: a twin-tailed comet, the divine symbol of the God-King, an announcement to all who beheld them that here were Sigmar's mightiest warriors – the Stormcast Eternals.

Reaching to his helm, one of the Stormcasts removed the mask he wore. The countenance locked behind the sigmarite metal was revealed as handsome and cultured. His black beard had a rakish cut and his dark hair was tied back in a plaited braid. There was a severity about the set of his jaw and a troubled cast to his pale grey eyes. With a flourish, the warrior swept his sapphire-hued cloak across his back and knelt upon the ground. His mailed fist reached to the earth, seized a handful of soil and brought it up to his nose. He closed his eyes and took a deep breath.

A tall Stormcast approached the warrior smelling his handful of earth. 'Something is amiss, Knight-Incantor?'

Knight-Incantor Arnhault of the Hammers of Sigmar opened his eyes and stared at his interrogator. 'No, Penthius,' he replied. 'We have indeed descended upon the realm of Ghur. The earth carries the smell of its magic.'

The Sequitor-Prime, Penthius, merely bowed his head. Arnhault was far more versed in the strange laws that governed the storm of magic and its disparate winds. Each of the Mortal Realms was governed by those winds, drawing more heavily from one than all the others combined to define its shape. 'Have you any way of knowing how far we might be from our objective?'

Arnhault let the soil sift through his fingers. There was a faint suggestion of a smile on his face. 'There is a familiar quality to its aura. Something that tells me we are not so very far from where we need to be.'

'Then I shall call your command together,' Penthius said. 'The sooner they are assembled and organised the more–' He cut his words short and stifled a colourful oath. Through the dissipating fog, gold-and-blue-armoured warriors bearing hefty greatbows dispersed between the trees. 'Nerio,' he grumbled. 'Already he breaks with protocol and indulges his whims.'

'The Castigator-Prime would call it instinct,' Arnhault reminded Penthius. 'There is more to strategy than the strictures laid down in tome and treatise. There are times when it is prudent to attend to what one *feels* rather than what one *knows*.'

Penthius shook his head. 'Instinct attends to but one possibility while doctrine seeks a plan flexible enough to confront many possibilities. Nerio's Castigators will be exposed the way he has deployed them. They will not have my Sequitors to guard them. We should adopt a block formation with the–'

Penthius' speech fell into an abrupt silence. Through the forest, a great rumbling could be heard. It took some moments before the noise became distinct enough to be discerned: the cracking of tree trunks and the crash of mighty boles against the earth. There were great pounding impacts as well, as though an avalanche were rolling through the woods.

One of the Castigators, his helm adorned with a great spiked halo, shouted from the periphery of the clearing. 'Knight-Incantor! Something approaches our position!'

'Pull your warriors back, Nerio!' Penthius shouted. 'If there is an enemy come to oppose us, my Sequitors will unleash Sigmar's storm with hammer and shield while your Castigators put a volley into them.'

'Keep your warriors where they are, Nerio,' Arnhault counter-manded. 'There is no time to redeploy. We must face the foe from the ground on which we stand.'

The rumbling in the forest was growing louder and seemed to have gathered impetus. The crack and crash of trees was ever more rapid. Now there could be felt tremors that shivered through the ground each time the pounding impacts slammed home. Arnhault knew what it meant, the terrible regularity of those impacts. They were the footfalls of some horrendously immense creature.

'Hammers of Sigmar! Brothers! Whatever comes, it will not stand between us and our duty to the God-King!' Arnhault raised his staff of office, letting its runes catch the fitful light drifting through the fog. At the sight of the Knight-Incantor's staff, a thundering war cry issued forth from the Stormcasts. 'Glory to the Heldenhammer!'

The defiant shouts of the Stormcasts enraged whatever moved through the forest. The violent charge picked up yet more speed. The tremors shaking the ground became a steady shudder. Trees leapt upwards as they were ripped from their roots and thrown into the sky. A heavy, musky stink spilled down into the clearing and caused such small animals as remained in their holes after the stormstrike to flee deeper into the forest.

Trees bordering the clearing were knocked asunder, crashing groundwards and forcing several of the Castigators to scramble from their path. In a spray of splinters and pine needles, a colossal shape emerged from the forest.

Towering over the Stormcasts and even many of the trees, the creature was covered in thick, shaggy black fur that was matted into twisted tangles and clotted with dried gore. Each of its four pillar-like legs was covered in a pebbly crimson skin, and its feet were broad pads with thick, plate-like toes. It had a large hump behind its short, thick neck – a slab of fatty tissue that was almost bald at its very top. The head of the creature was long and broad, with a wide mouth and enormous ebony tusks that curled back upon themselves. Its eyes were small and sharp, clouded with a scarlet sheen of frenzied fury. From the front of its face, a long snake-like trunk sagged and swayed – at least until its beady eyes sighted Knight-Incantor Arnhault. Then the creature reared up on its hind legs and raised its trunk to the sky. A deafening trumpet sounded from the mammoth, and when its tremendous bulk slammed back down onto all four legs, the tremor was such that Arnhault could feel it pulse through his bones.

He could also sense the malign energies that exuded from the creature. It was at once more and less than a mere beast of Ghur. The corrupt touch of Chaos was upon it, twisting it in both body and spirit. Arnhault felt its pain – the mammoth was wracked by the torment of isolation and consumed by a fratricidal madness that had caused it to slaughter its own herd. The bloodlust of Khorne ran through its gigantic frame, manifesting outwardly in spiky knobs of bone that protruded from its shaggy pelt. When the beast trumpeted a second time he detected a belligerence beyond that of a simple animal, rather the fury of a thing lost and damned.

Anger pulsed through Arnhault's veins – not the blind fury of Chaos but the righteous indignation of Sigmar. In his mind's eye he saw an image of what the mammoth should have been, a vision of the magnificent creature before it had been corrupted. Memories flickered before him of great herds of shaggy giants striding across autumnal plains, lending their mighty strength to the last harvest of the inhabitants in return for bushels of fruits and bundles of spring sweet grass. Those mammoths had been wise and gentle, far removed from the crazed beast that now opposed the Stormcasts.

'I will end this torment,' Arnhault vowed, staring into the beast's red eyes. He raised his staff, drawing upon the magic of the storm.

The mammoth bellowed once more and charged towards the Knight-Incantor. The instant it started to move, the Castigators arrayed around it began to shoot. The bulky thunderhead greatbows roared as they loosed a deadly barrage into the immense beast. Mace-like quarrels slammed into the shaggy hide, their crystalline heads exploding in bursts of celestial energy. The condensed breath of Stardrakes was sent crackling across the mammoth's body, searing its fur and scalding its skin. In a heartbeat, the bulky feeder atop each greatbow set another mace into place and the Castigators sent another volley into the raging beast.

A nimbus of light flared from Arnhault's staff as he swept it towards the mammoth. Flung from its head, the light expanded to become a withering wind, hot as the stars and cold as the void. The stellar storm swept across the charging beast, and in that arcane gale its shaggy pelt was peeled back, ripped from its hide in ragged clumps and gory strips. The denuded skin beneath was scarred and wet with blood, pock-marked with the malignant mutations of Chaos. Obscene growths quivered and writhed with loathsome animation as the divine wind ravaged the beast.

The wind Arnhault had drawn down into his staff was enough to bring a gargant to its knees, but the ferocity of the mammoth was such that it thundered onwards, refusing to be bowed despite the magnitude of its injuries. The very gore that bubbled from its wounds gave the beast renewed strength, for the Blood God did not care overmuch from whence the blood flowed.

'Sequitors! Shield and hammer!' Penthius' commanding tone rang out across the clearing. At a run, a dozen warriors stood between the mammoth and Arnhault. Swinging their broad shields before them as the beast pounded forwards, the Sequitors raised their stormsmite mauls. Blue energy crackled about the head of each weapon, an aura of power drawn from the very essence of Azyr, the God-King's realm. Before the mammoth reached their line, that blue glow was drawn away from the hammers, passing instead into the gilded faces of their soulshields.

When the mammoth struck the line of Sequitors, a titanic shudder swept across the clearing and knocked branches from the outlying trees. Coruscant energies flittered through the air, crackling away in a dazzling display of power. Incredibly, the Sequitors held their ground, their line unbroken. Before them, the giant beast stood swaying from side to side, stunned by the calamitous impact of its charging bulk upon the nigh-impenetrable bulwark of the soulshields.

'Castigators! Loose!' Nerio raised his own greatbow and sent thunderhead maces exploding against the mammoth's flanks. Again the condensed Stardrake's breath was sent searing across the beast's mutated frame.

'Hammer and shield!' Penthius shouted to his own warriors. With the command, the glow left the soulshields and once more infused the heavy mauls the Sequitors bore. As arcane energy crackled about their weapons, the Stormcasts brought them crashing against the mammoth's pillar-like legs and tusked head. Flesh sizzled under their blows. Teeth were shattered in the beast's jaw. Blood turned to steam as it spurted across the glowing hammers.

Yet still the mammoth did not fall. Trumpeting its rage, its trunk coiled around one of the Sequitors. With acute awareness, the beast chose Penthius for its victim, pulling the Sequitor-Prime from the very midst of his Stormcasts. It lifted him into the air, his sigmarite armour creaking as the creature's trunk curled itself into a crushing grip.

Before the mammoth could destroy its captive, a thunder-head mace exploded against its trunk. Nerio, alerted to Penthius' danger, sent the shot slamming into the base of the extremity with unerring accuracy, the missile streaking past the curl of the tusks to detonate against the beast's face. A great mass of flesh and sinew was blasted away by the con-centrated Stardrake's breath. All animation fled from the mammoth's trunk as it sagged limply against the ground. Penthius rolled clear of the lifeless coils and brought his maul cracking against one of the tusks. A jagged crack rippled through the ivory, and the mammoth reared back in shock.

'It is time to end your torture,' Arnhault intoned. For all that the mammoth was a crazed and corrupt beast of Chaos, he could not feel anything but regret for the pain his retinue had inflicted upon it. The most merciful thing that could be extended to the beast was the oblivion of a swift death. His voice dipped into a low cadence, invoking the spells of the Sacrosanct Chamber and the lore of High Azyr. A different light gathered about the staff he bore, a pearlescent glow that rippled with celestial power.

'Spirits of storm and sky, let your wrath flow through me.' Arnhault gestured with his staff and the glow leapt from its length, stretching out to become a flash of lightning. The unleashed energy struck against the mammoth's forehead, searing a black hole into its skull. The beast reared up, one foreleg kicking at the air, and then it came crashing down. The impact of its fall sent a shudder through the forest.

Smoke rose from the hole Arnhault's magic had burned

into the mammoth's head, yet still the beast clung stubbornly to life. Its eyes retained a berserk fury as they focused upon the Knight-Incantor. Arnhault shook his head. He could not hate this beast any more than he could hate a rabid dog. It was a sick and maddened thing, a creature that had to be destroyed out of necessity. It was pity, not ire, that caused him to turn towards the Sequitors. 'Orthan,' he called out. 'Deliver Sigmar's rest.'

From amidst the ranks of the Sequitors a lone warrior marched forwards. Though armoured in the gold and blue of his brothers, Orthan had forsaken the maul and shield they bore. Instead he carried an immense mace, a weapon with a haft as long as the Stormcast was tall. The head of the weapon was a black bludgeon of enchanted sigmarite through which flickers of divine power flashed. Runes and sigils extolling the might of the God-King were etched across the dark surface and about its neck was a band of purest gold adorned with the emblem of the Hammer, holy Ghal Maraz itself.

Orthan advanced upon the fallen mammoth and halted beside the beast's smouldering head. 'For Sigmar!' the Sequitor howled as he lifted the stormsmite greatmace upwards. The flickers of divine power became a halo of might, suffusing the weapon and the warrior who held it. In a single stroke, Orthan brought the bludgeon crashing downwards. As its smashed into the mammoth's skull, pebbly flesh thick as a man's palm evaporated, inches of skull reduced to crackling cinders. An instant only, and the mammoth's head was reduced to ash. The beast's enormous frame quivered in a final spasm of pain and then was still.

While Orthan visited death upon the mammoth, Arnhault drew a silver vial from a pouch on his belt. An arcane song of eternity whispered across his lips as he held the vessel towards the beast. The instant the creature's life was driven from it, the magic he evoked reached out to the fleeing spirit. He could feel the Chaos contamination drifting apart from the core of the beast's essence, and it was this essence that his spell ensnared. With fingers of aetheric force, Arnhault's magic drew the mammoth's spirit down into the vial, pouring it into the tiny vessel until it was filled with the boiling energies of the vanquished giant. Only when he was certain he had drawn all that remained uncorrupted did Arnhault bring his song to an end. For a moment he could actually see the dark belligerence of Chaos lingering above the mammoth's carcass. Then it began to fade, seeping back into the cursed regions from whence it had come.

Arnhault stared at the vial for a moment and then quickly pressed a sigmarite stopper into the neck of the vessel. A powerful rune fashioned by duardin demi-gods adorned the underside of the stopper, forming a barrier no spirit could penetrate.

Castigator-Prime Nerio approached Arnhault as he returned the vial to the pouch on his belt. 'Forgive my impertinence, Knight-Incantor, but is it wise to try to trap such a spirit?'

Arnhault tapped his fingers against the pouch. 'For all the enormity of its flesh, the beast's spirit is a simple thing. Were it otherwise the taint of Chaos would have befouled it as completely as it defiled its body.' He shook his head. 'No, it is no reckless testing of my arts which you have beheld, merely a practical application of knowledge you too may prove worthy to learn.'

'Nerio would first need to learn how to confine himself to the structure of his lessons.' Penthius walked around the dead bulk of the mammoth to join his brothers. 'I do not think it would be prudent to train an acolyte who insists on learning how to conjure magic before he knows how to safely dispel it.'

The Castigator-Prime rounded on Penthius. 'A versatile mind understands the difference between recklessness and initiative.'

'Yes,' Penthius agreed. 'A versatile mind *does*.'

Nerio patted the thunderhead greatbow slung over his shoulder. 'If I were not versatile that beast would have twisted your armour into such a state that you would now pass for a marsh crab.'

'If you had kept your archers in formation, we could have settled with the brute before it got to grips with anyone,' Penthius growled back at him. 'It is not for nothing that established procedures are observed. At least by a disciplined warrior.'

Arnhault interjected himself into what he knew would swell into bitter argument if allowed to escalate. Many times he had undertaken missions with Penthius and Nerio in his retinue, but never had he seen them agree upon anything when it came to tactics. Penthius was too hidebound and rigid, doggedly adhering to martial tradition. Nerio, by contrast, was impulsive and headstrong.

'We will save the tactical discussion for a later time,' Arnhault decreed. It was all he needed to say. If there was one thing Penthius and Nerio could agree upon, it was the depth of their loyalty to the Knight-Incantor. When Arnhault gave an order, it was obeyed instantly. The disagreement was forgotten until fresh provocation caused it to return.

Penthius turned towards the Knight-Incantor and bowed his head in deference to Arnhault's rank. 'Your knowledge of Ghur is formidable. Have you any awareness of this place? Do you know how near we may be to where our duty would take us?'

Arnhault's eyes closed as he considered the questions posed to him. 'We stand now in what was once the Wood of Gyr.' He looked to the trees from whence the mammoth had emerged. 'There is a crispness to the air in that direction, a trace of ice on the breeze. If we were to travel that way, we should find Frostmoor and its screaming glaciers. Long ago, it would have been a journey of many days' march.' Arnhault gestured to the pines that dominated the forest around them. 'But I speak of when the Wood of Gyr was home to willow and palm. The land has changed. As the screaming glaciers crawl further from Frostmoor, they drive the beasts and plants of the taiga before them.' He pointed his sigmarite staff at the mammoth's carcass. 'There was a time when these beasts were unknown in Gyr and rare in the Kingdom of Kharza.'

'Kharza is near then?' Nerio asked.

'It is near enough,' Arnhault supplied. 'The royal house of Kharza would ride to the Wood of Gyr to honour the Rites of Taal and hunt the golden boar with jade-tipped spears and sacred leopards trained to hunt no other prey. Their entourages would spend a fortnight travelling to the hunt and back.' He swung around and nodded towards the trees to his right. 'The journey will take us less time,' he stated. 'We are not encumbered by the regalia of royalty and the baggage of the hunt.'

'For all that, we too are hunters,' Nerio said. He reached to the quiver of crystal-headed maces that hung at his side.

'We are not hunters,' Penthius corrected him. 'We are protectors. Our duty is not to simply track some wild brute to its lair. An appeal has been made and that prayer has been heard. We are come to save the faithful of Wyrmditt from the evil that besets them.' He looked back to the mutated mammoth. 'Evil far different to the beasts of Chaos, but no less deadly.'

Nerio shook his head. 'It will not be enough to defend these people. We will have to root out this menace and destroy it utterly if we would bring them a lasting peace. Make no mistake, brother, we are hunters.'

'We are neither protectors nor hunters,' Arnhault said. He donned his helm, locking his face once more behind the stern metal mask. 'We are avengers,' he told his warriors. 'We come not simply to bring relief to the people of Wyrmditt. We will confront the darkness that threatens them and we will make it answer for its manifold outrages.'

Arnhault gestured to his brothers. 'Get our warriors into formation. Nerio, you will abide by whatever deployment Penthius deems advisable. Penthius, you will allow the Castigators flexibility of action should we encounter any unexpected obstacles.' He indicated the mammoth. 'Even before the scourge of Chaos threatened to overwhelm it utterly, Ghur was a place of fearsome beasts. With monsters twisted by the Dark Gods roaming the land, we must be doubly vigilant.

'Wyrmditt lies beyond the Wood of Gyr, across the veldt of the Fangfields and the hill country of Takrahn.' Arnhault nodded to himself as he envisioned the maps he had consulted when this duty had been entrusted to him, matching the place names to his more exacting knowledge. 'The town is deep within one of the border marches of Kharza, at the very edge of the old fiefdoms.'

'That is why the people are imperilled,' Penthius stated. 'They are too near the fallen kingdom. Too close to the shadows of the past.'

Arnhault gave the Sequitor-Prime a reproachful look. 'The

shadows of the past hang over us all, brother.' He swept his gaze across the clearing, studying the forest around them. 'Perhaps the past is never a heavier burden than when we do not recognise its weight upon us.'

Mouldering darkness filled the silent hall. The pomp and pageantry of the court was absent now, and in their place there was only an oppressive gloom.

Sabrodt leaned back into the diamond-headed throne. Golden wings cast to echo the leathery pinions of dragons formed a magnificent canopy overhead. The heavy arms of the throne were like scaly coils; the broad feet were clawed talons. If he raised his eyes he could see the fanged visage of the dragon, the huge diamond lodged in its throat. In the right light, an eerie flicker shimmered within the diamond, as though the beast's flame were about to spill forth and immolate those who bowed before the throne.

Since his early childhood, Sabrodt had been enthralled by the Dragonseat. He was captivated by its wondrous beauty, the richness of its settings and the craftsmanship that infused every curve and line, each scale and claw, with masterful artistry. Nowhere, he was convinced, was there anything so grand as this throne. Not in the palaces of the gods themselves could such magnificence possibly be found.

The royal court's splendour was as nothing when compared to the Dragonseat. Artisans from lands beyond a hundred horizons had laboured to create a hall that could complement the throne at its centre. No feat of man or duardin had been equal to the task. Sabrodt had watched them fail, one after another, led away in disgrace to the priest-king's dungeons. As a boy, he had gone down to those benighted vaults to listen to the artists bewailing their fate, begging their guards for even one more glimpse of the masterpiece they had failed to match.

How he had longed to sit upon the Dragonseat and to possess it. Being so near to it year upon year had been a kind of torture to Sabrodt. Always so close, always within reach. Yet he could not dare to reach, for only the priest-king was allowed to touch the throne.

A grisly laugh rose from Sabrodt. Now. Now he *was* priest-king.

His gaze pierced the darkness of the hall, for there was no shadow that could hide its secrets from him any more. He could see the cracked pillars of malachite and obsidian that ringed the chamber, the archways of black marble that stretched between them and helped support the ceiling. Mouldy tatters of tapestry yet clung to the archways, hanging like dusty cobwebs. The lavish rugs that stretched across the floor were faded and frayed, clotted with dirt and grime. The tile frescoes adorning the walls were cracked and crumbling, exposing the grey earth behind them.

The grisly laugh took on a bitter note as Sabrodt stared at the jumbled bones piled about the chamber. It was many years since the court of Kharza had been as he remembered it. The morbid stamp of death was upon it now.

Sabrodt leaned back in the Dragonseat, the throne he had coveted for so very long, and his insubstantial spirit shifted through the ancient chair. He was priest-king, lord of Kharza and the only one with the authority to sit upon the throne, yet it was the one thing he could not do. Only by the greatest exertion of willpower could he impel some semblance of solidity to his being. But to touch the Dragonseat was a thing too keenly desired, too dearly cherished. The moment he tried, his focus would be lost and his phantom hand would pass right through the throne.

A spiteful snarl hissed its way through Sabrodt's fleshless face. He rose from the throne and drew his ragged burial shroud closer around his spectral form. The Dragonseat was a foolishness of his youth, the idle dream of a child. It was not the throne he had coveted. It was the power it represented. The power he now commanded. He, *he* was priest-king!

Ghostly lights blazed within the hollows of the wraith's skull. Kharza belonged to Sabrodt. It was his dominion and would be forever. That was the promise Black Nagash made to him when he had sworn his soul to the Great Necromancer.

That was the curse that would not allow Sabrodt to rest quiet in his grave.

Sabrodt, priest-king of Kharza.

Sabrodt, the Shrouded King.

YOUR
NEXT READ

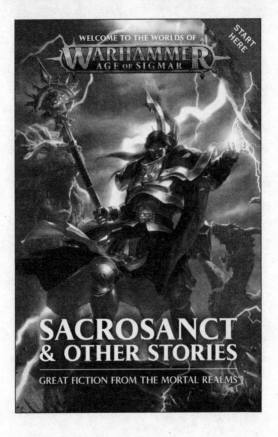

SACROSANCT & OTHER STORIES
by various authors

Enjoy a collection of tales from the Mortal Realms, covering a host of races and factions and providing a taste of the flavour of the Age of Sigmar.

WARHAMMER®
CHRONICLES

TROLLSLAYER

WILLIAM KING

'Damn all manling coach drivers and all manling women,'
Gotrek Gurnisson muttered, adding a curse in dwarfish.

'You did have to insult the lady Isolde, didn't you?' Felix
Jaeger said peevishly. 'As things are, we're lucky they didn't
just shoot us. If you can call it "lucky" to be dumped in the
Reikwald on Geheimnisnacht Eve.'

'We paid for our passage. We were just as entitled to sit
inside as her. The drivers were unmanly cowards,' Gotrek
grumbled. 'They refused to meet me hand to hand. I would
not have minded being spitted on steel, but being blasted
with buckshot is no death for a Trollslayer.'

Felix shook his head. He could see that one of his companion's black moods was coming on. There would be no
arguing with him and Felix had plenty of other things to
worry about. The sun was setting, giving the mist-covered
forest a ruddy hue.

Long shadows danced eerily and brought to mind too

many frightening tales of the horrors to be found under the canopy of trees.

He wiped his nose with the edge of his cloak, then pulled the Sudenland wool tight about him. He sniffed and looked at the sky where Morrslieb and Mannslieb, the lesser and greater moons, were already visible. Morrslieb seemed to be giving off a faint greenish glow. It wasn't a good sign.

'I think I have a fever coming on,' Felix said. The Trollslayer looked up at him and chuckled contemptuously. In the last rays of the dying sun, his nose-chain was a bloody arc running from nostril to ear-lobe.

'Yours is a weak race,' Gotrek said. 'The only fever I feel this eve is the battle-fever. It sings in my head.'

He turned and glared out into the darkness of the woods. 'Come out, little beastmen!' he bellowed. 'I have a gift for you.'

He laughed loudly and ran his thumb along the edge of the blade of his great two-handed axe. Felix saw that it drew blood. Gotrek began to suck his thumb.

'Sigmar preserve us, be quiet!' Felix hissed. 'Who knows what lurks out there on a night like this?'

Gotrek glared at him. Felix could see the glint of insane violence appear in his eyes. Instinctively Felix's hand strayed nearer to the pommel of his sword.

'Give me no orders, manling! I am of the Elder Race and am beholden only to the Kings Under the Mountain, exile though I be.'

Felix bowed formally. He was well schooled in the use of the sword. The scars on his face showed that he had fought several duels in his student days. He had once killed a man and so ended a promising academic career. But still he did not relish the thought of fighting the Trollslayer. The tip of

Gotrek's crested hair came only to the level of Felix's chest, but the dwarf outweighed him and his bulk was all muscle. And Felix had seen Gotrek use that axe.

The dwarf took the bow as an apology and turned once more to the darkness. 'Come out!' he shouted. 'I care not if all the powers of evil walk the woods this night. I will face any challenger.'

The dwarf was working himself up to a pitch of fury. During the time of their acquaintance Felix had noticed that the Trollslayer's long periods of brooding were often followed by brief explosions of rage. It was one of the things about his companion that fascinated Felix. He knew that Gotrek had become a Trollslayer to atone for some crime. He was sworn to seek death in unequal combat with fearsome monsters. He seemed bitter to the point of madness – yet he kept to his oath.

Perhaps, thought Felix, I too would go mad if I had been driven into exile among strangers not even of my own race. He felt some sympathy for the crazed dwarf. Felix knew what it was like to be driven from home under a cloud. The duel with Wolfgang Krassner had caused quite a scandal.

At that moment, however, the dwarf seemed bent on getting them both killed, and he wanted no part of it. Felix continued to plod along the road, casting an occasional worried glance at the bright full moons. Behind him the ranting continued.

'Are there no warriors among you? Come feel my axe. She thirsts!'

Only a madman would so tempt fate and the dark powers on Geheimnisnacht, Night of Mystery, in the darkest reaches of the forest, Felix decided.

He could make out chanting in the flinty, guttural tongue of the Mountain Dwarfs, then once more in Reikspiel, he heard: 'Send me a champion!'

For a second there was silence. Condensation from the clammy mist ran down his brow. Then – from far, far off – the sound of galloping horses rang out in the quiet night.

What has that maniac done, Felix thought, has he offended one of the Old Powers? Have they sent their daemon riders to carry us off?

Felix stepped off the road. He shuddered as wet leaves fondled his face. They felt like dead men's fingers. The thunder of hooves came closer, moving with hellish speed along the forest road. Surely only a supernatural being could keep such breakneck pace on the winding forest road? He felt his hand shake as he unsheathed his sword.

I was foolish to follow Gotrek, he thought. Now I'll never get the poem finished. He could hear the loud neighing of horses, the cracking of a whip and mighty wheels turning.

'Good!' Gotrek roared. His voice drifted from the trail behind. 'Good!'

There was a loud bellowing and four immense jet black horses drawing an equally black coach hurtled past. Felix saw the wheels bounce as they hit a rut in the road. He could just make out a black-cloaked driver. He shrank back into the bushes.

He heard the sound of feet coming closer. The bushes were pulled aside. Before him stood Gotrek, looking madder and wilder than ever. His crest was matted, brown mud was smeared over his tattooed body and his studded leather jerkin was ripped and torn.

'The snotling-fondlers tried to run me over!' he yelled. 'Let's get after them!'

He turned and headed up the muddy road at a fast trot. Felix noted that Gotrek was singing happily in Khazalid.

Further down the Bogenhafen road the pair found the Standing Stones Inn. The windows were shuttered and no lights showed. They could hear a neighing from the stables but when they checked there was no coach, black or otherwise, only some skittish ponies and a peddler's cart.

'We've lost the coach. Might as well get a bed for the night,' Felix suggested. He looked warily at the smaller moon, Morrslieb. The sickly green glow was stronger. 'I do not like being abroad under this evil light.'

'You are feeble, manling. Cowardly too.'

'They'll have ale.'

'On the other hand, some of your suggestions are not without merit. Watery though human beer is, of course.'

'Of course,' Felix said. Gotrek failed to spot the note of irony in his voice.

The inn was not fortified but the walls were thick, and when they tried the door they found it was barred. Gotrek began to bang it with the butt of his axe-shaft. There was no response.

'I can smell humans within,' Gotrek said. Felix wondered how he could smell anything over his own stench. Gotrek never washed and his hair was matted with animal fat to keep his red-dyed crest in place.

'They'll have locked themselves in. Nobody goes abroad on Geheimnisnacht. Unless they're witches or daemon-lovers.'

'The black coach was abroad,' Gotrek said.

'Its occupants were up to no good. The windows were curtained and the coach bore no crest of arms.'

'My throat is too dry to discuss such details. Come on, open up in there or I'll take my axe to the door!'

Felix thought he heard movement within. He pressed an ear to the door. He could make out the mutter of voices and what sounded like weeping.

'Unless you want me to chop through your head, manling, I suggest you stand aside,' Gotrek said to Felix.

'Just a moment. I say: you inside! Open up! My friend has a very large axe and a very short temper. I suggest you do as he says or lose your door.'

'What was that about "short"?' Gotrek said touchily.

From behind the door came a thin, quavering cry. 'In the name of Sigmar, begone, you daemons of the pit!'

'Right, that's it,' Gotrek snapped. 'I've had enough.'

He drew his axe back in a huge arc. Felix saw the runes on its blade gleam in the Morrslieb light. He leapt aside.

'In the name of Sigmar!' Felix shouted. 'You cannot exorcise us. We are simple, weary travellers.'

The axe bit into the door with a chunking sound. Splinters of wood flew from it. Gotrek turned to Felix and grinned evilly up at him. Felix noted the missing teeth.

'Shoddily made, these manling doors,' Gotrek said.

'I suggest you open up while you still have a door,' Felix called.

'Wait,' the quavering voice said. 'That door cost me five crowns from Jurgen the carpenter.'

The door was unlatched. It opened. A tall, thin man with a sad face framed by lank, white hair stood there. He had a stout club in one hand. Behind him stood an old woman who held a saucer that contained a guttering candle.

'You will not need your weapon, sir. We require only a bed for the night,' Felix said.

'And ale,' the dwarf grunted.

'And ale,' Felix agreed.

'Lots of ale,' Gotrek said. Felix looked at the old man and shrugged helplessly.

Inside, the inn had a low common room. The bar was made of planks stretched across two barrels. From the corner, three armed men who looked like travelling peddlers watched them warily. They each had daggers drawn. The shadows hid their faces but they seemed worried.

The innkeeper hustled the pair inside and slid the bars back into place. 'Can you pay, Herr Doktor?' he asked nervously. Felix could see the man's Adam's apple moving.

'I am not a professor, I am a poet,' he said, producing his thin pouch and counting out his few remaining gold coins. 'But I can pay.'

'Food,' Gotrek said. 'And ale.'

At this the old woman burst into tears. Felix stared at her.

'The hag is discomfited,' Gotrek said.

The old man nodded. 'Our Gunter is missing, on this of all nights.'

'Get me some ale,' Gotrek said. The innkeeper backed off. Gotrek got up and stumped over to where the peddlers were sitting. They regarded him warily.

'Do any of you know about a black coach drawn by four black horses?' Gotrek asked.

'You have seen the black coach?' one of the peddlers asked. The fear was evident in his voice.

'Seen it? The bloody thing nearly ran me over.' A man gasped. Felix heard the sound of a ladle being dropped. He saw the innkeeper stoop to pick it up and begin refilling the tankard.

'You are lucky then,' the fattest and most prosperous-looking peddler said. 'Some say the coach is driven by daemons. I have heard it passes here on Geheimnisnacht every year. Some say it carries wee children from Altdorf who are sacrificed at the Darkstone Ring.'

Gotrek looked at him with interest. Felix did not like the way this was developing.

'Surely that is only a legend,' he said.

'No, sir,' the innkeeper shouted. 'Every year we hear the thunder of its passing. Two years ago Gunter looked out and saw it, a black coach just as you describe.'

At the mention of Gunter's name the old woman began to cry again. The innkeeper brought stew and two great steins of ale.

'Bring beer for my companion too,' Gotrek said. The landlord went off for another stein.

'Who is Gunter?' Felix asked when he returned. There was another wail from the old woman.

'More ale,' Gotrek said. The landlord looked in astonishment at the empty flagons.

'Take mine,' Felix said. 'Now, mein host, who is Gunter?'

'And why does the old hag howl at the very mention of his name?' Gotrek asked, wiping his mouth on his mud-encrusted arm.

'Gunter is our son. He went out to chop wood this afternoon. He has not returned.'

'Gunter is a good boy,' the old woman sniffled. 'How will we survive without him?'

'Perhaps he is simply lost in the woods?'

'Impossible,' the innkeeper said. 'Gunter knows the woods round here like I know the hairs on my hand. He should have been home hours ago. I fear the coven has taken him, as a sacrifice.'

'It's just like Lotte Hauptmann's daughter, Ingrid,' the fat peddler said. The innkeeper shot him a dirty look.

'I want no tales told of our son's betrothed,' he said.

'Let the man speak,' Gotrek said. The peddler looked at him gratefully.

'The same thing happened last year, in Hartzroch, just down the road. Goodwife Hauptmann looked in on her teenage daughter Ingrid just after sunset. She thought she heard banging coming from her daughter's room. The girl was gone, snatched by who-knows-what sorcerous power from her bed in a locked house. The next day the hue and cry went up. We found Ingrid. She was covered in bruises and in a terrible state.'

He looked at them to make sure he had their attention. 'You asked her what happened?' Felix said.

'Aye, sir. It seems she had been carried off by daemons, wild things of the wood, to Darkstone Ring. There the coven waited with evil creatures from the forests. They made to sacrifice her at the altar but she broke free from her captors and invoked the good name of blessed Sigmar. While they reeled she fled. They pursued her but could not overtake her.'

'That was lucky,' Felix said dryly.

'There is no need to mock, Herr Doktor. We made our way to the stones and we did find all sorts of tracks in the disturbed earth. Including those of humans and beasts and cloven-hoofed daemons. And a yearling infant gutted like a pig upon the altar.'

'Cloven-hoofed daemons?' Gotrek asked. Felix didn't like the look of interest in his eye. The peddler nodded.

'I would not venture up to Darkstone Ring tonight,' the peddler said. 'Not for all the gold in Altdorf.'

'It would be a task fit for a hero,' Gotrek said, looking meaningfully at Felix. Felix was shocked.

'Surely you cannot mean–'

'What better task for a Trollslayer than to face these daemons on their sacred night? It would be a mighty death.'

'It would be a stupid death,' Felix muttered.

'What was that?'

'Nothing.'

'You are coming, aren't you?' Gotrek said menacingly. He was rubbing his thumb along the blade of his axe. Felix noticed that it was bleeding again.

He nodded slowly. 'An oath is an oath.'

The dwarf slapped him upon the back with such force that he thought his ribs would break. 'Sometimes, manling, I think you must have dwarf blood in you. Not that any of the Elder race would stoop to such a mixed marriage, of course.'

He stomped back to his ale.

'Of course,' his companion said, glaring at his back.

Felix fumbled in his pack for his mail shirt. He noticed that the innkeeper and his wife and the peddlers were looking at him. Their eyes held something that looked close to awe. Gotrek sat near the fire drinking ale and grumbling in dwarfish.

'You're not really going with him?' the fat peddler whispered. Felix nodded.

'Why?'

'He saved my life. I owe him a debt.' Felix thought it best not to mention the circumstances under which Gotrek had saved him.

'I pulled the manling out from under the hooves of the Emperor's cavalry,' Gotrek shouted.

Felix cursed bitterly. The Trollslayer has the hearing of a wild beast as well as the brains of one, he thought to himself, continuing to pull on the mail shirt.

'Aye. The manling thought it clever to put his case to the Emperor with petitions and protest marches. Old Karl Franz chose to respond, quite sensibly, with cavalry charges.'

The peddlers were starting to back away.

'An insurrectionist,' Felix heard one mutter.

Felix felt his face flush. 'It was yet another cruel and unjust tax. A silver piece for every window, indeed. To make it worse, all the fat merchants bricked up their windows and the Alt-dorf militia went around knocking holes in the side of poor folks' hovels. We were right to speak out.'

'There's a reward for the capture of insurrectionists,' the peddler said. 'A big reward.'

Felix stared at him. 'Of course, the Imperial cavalry were no match for my companion's axe,' he said. 'Such carnage! Heads, legs, arms everywhere. He stood on a pile of bodies.'

'They called for archers,' Gotrek said. 'We departed down a back alley. Being spitted from afar would have been an unseemly death.'

The fat peddler looked at his companions then at Gotrek, then at Felix, then back at his companions. 'A sensible man keeps out of politics,' he said to the man who had talked of rewards. He looked at Felix. 'No offence, sir.'

'None taken,' Felix said. 'You are absolutely correct.'

'Insurrectionist or no,' the old woman said, 'may Sigmar bless you if you bring my little Gunter back.'

'He is not little, Lise,' the innkeeper said. 'He is a strapping young man. Still, I hope you bring my son back. I am old and I need him to chop the wood and shoe the horses and lift the kegs and–'

'I am touched by your paternal concern, sir,' Felix interrupted. He pulled his leather cap down on his head.

Gotrek got up and looked at him. He beat his chest with

one meaty hand. 'Armour is for women and girly elves,' he said.

'Perhaps I had best wear it, Gotrek. If I am to return alive with the tale of your deeds – as I did, after all, swear to do.'

'You have a point, manling. And remember that is not all you swore to do.' He turned to the innkeeper. 'How will we find the Darkstone Ring?'

Felix felt his mouth go dry. He fought to keep his hands from shaking.

'There is a trail. It runs from the road. I will take you to its start.'

'Good,' Gotrek said. 'This is too good an opportunity to miss. Tonight I will atone my sins and stand among the Iron Halls of my fathers. Great Grungni willing.'

He made a peculiar sign over his chest with his clenched right hand. 'Come, manling, let us go.' He strode out the door.

Felix picked up his pack. At the doorway the old woman stopped him and pressed something into his hand. 'Please, sir,' she said. 'Take this. It is a charm to Sigmar. It will protect you. My little Gunter wears its twin.'

And much good it's done him, Felix was about to say, but the expression on her face stopped him. It held fear, concern and perhaps hope. He was touched.

'I'll do my best, frau.'

Outside, the sky was bright with the green witchlight of the moons. Felix opened his hand. In it was a small iron hammer on a fine-linked chain. He shrugged and hung it round his neck. Gotrek and the old man were already moving down the road. He had to run to catch up.

'What do you think these are, manling?' Gotrek said, bending close to the ground. Ahead of them, the road continued on towards Hartzroch and Bogenhafen. Felix leaned on the league marker. This was the edge of the trail. Felix hoped the innkeeper had returned home safely.

'Tracks,' he said. 'Going north.'

'Very good, manling. They are coach tracks and they take the trail north to the Darkstone Ring.'

'The black coach?' Felix said.

'I hope so. What a glorious night! All my prayers are answered. A chance to atone and to get revenge on the swine who nearly ran me over.' Gotrek cackled gleefully but Felix could sense a change in him. He seemed tense, as if suspecting that his hour of destiny were arriving and he would meet it badly. He seemed unusually talkative.

'A coach? Does this coven consist of noblemen, manling? Is your Empire so very corrupt?'

Felix shook his head. 'I don't know. It may have a noble leader. The members are most likely local folk. They say the taint of Chaos runs deep in these out of the way places.'

Gotrek shook his head and for the first time ever he looked dismayed. 'I could weep for the folly of your people, manling. To be so corrupted that your rulers could sell themselves over to the powers of darkness, that is a terrible thing.'

'Not all men are so,' Felix said angrily. 'True, some seek easy power or the pleasures of the flesh, but they are few. Most people keep the faith. Anyway, the Elder Race are not so pure. I have heard tales of whole armies of dwarfs dedicated to the Ruinous Powers.'

Gotrek gave a low angry growl and spat on the ground. Felix gripped the hilt of his sword tighter. He wondered whether he had pushed the Trollslayer too far.

'You are correct,' Gotrek said, his voice soft and cold. 'We do not lightly talk about such things. We have vowed eternal war against the abominations you mention and their dark masters.'

'As have my own people. We have our witch hunts and our laws.'

Gotrek shook his head. 'Your people do not understand. They are soft and decadent and live far from the war. They do not understand the terrible things which gnaw at the roots of the world and seek to undermine us all. Witch hunts? Hah!' He spat on the ground. 'Laws! There is only one way to meet the threat of Chaos.'

He brandished his axe meaningfully.

They trudged wearily through the forest. Overhead, the moons gleamed feverishly. Morrslieb had become ever brighter, and now its green glow stained the sky. A light mist had gathered and the terrain they moved through was bleak and wild. Rocks broke through the turf like plague spots breaking through the skin of the world.

Sometimes Felix thought he could hear great wings passing overhead, but when he looked up he could see only the glow in the sky. The mist distorted and spread so that it looked as though they walked along the bed of some infernal sea.

There was a sense of wrongness about this place, Felix decided. The air tasted foul and the hairs on the nape of his neck constantly prickled. Back when he had been a boy in Altdorf he had sat in his father's house and watched the sky grow black with menacing clouds. Then had come the most monstrous storm in living memory. Now he felt the same sense of anticipation. Mighty forces were gathering close to here, he was certain. He felt like an insect crawling over the body of a giant that could at any moment awake and crush him.

Even Gotrek seemed oppressed. He had fallen silent and

did not even mumble to himself as he usually did. Now and again he would stop and motion for Felix to stand quiet, then he would stand and sniff the air. Felix could see that his whole body tensed as if he strained with every nerve to catch the slightest trace of something. Then they would move on.

Felix's muscles all felt tight with tension. He wished he had not come. Surely, he told himself, my obligation to the dwarf does not mean I must face certain death. Perhaps I can slip away in the mist.

He gritted his teeth. He prided himself on being an honourable man, and the debt he owed the dwarf was real. The dwarf had risked his life to save him. Granted, at the time he had not known Gotrek was seeking death, courting it as a man courts a desirable lady. It still left him under an obligation.

He remembered the riotous drunken evening in the taverns of the Maze when they had sworn blood-brothership in that curious dwarfish rite and he had agreed to help Gotrek in his quest.

Gotrek wished his name remembered and his deeds recalled. When he had found out that Felix was a poet, the dwarf had asked Felix to accompany him. At the time, in the warm glow of beery camaraderie, it had seemed a splendid idea. The Trollslayer's doomed quest had struck Felix as excellent material for an epic poem, one that would make him famous.

Little did I know, Felix thought, that it would lead to this. Hunting for monsters on Geheimnisnacht. He smiled ironically. It was easy to sing of brave deeds in the taverns and playhalls where horror was a thing conjured by the words of skilled craftsmen. Out here, though, it was different. His bowels felt loose with fear and the oppressive atmosphere made him want to run screaming.

Still, he tried to console himself, this is fit subject matter for a poem. If only I live to write it.

The woods became deeper and more tangled. The trees took on the aspect of twisted, uncanny beings. Felix felt as if they were watching him. He tried to dismiss the thought as fantasy but the mist and the ghastly moonlight only stimulated his imagination. He felt as if every pool of shadow contained a monster.

Felix looked down at the dwarf. Gotrek's face held a mixture of anticipation and fear. Felix had thought him immune to terror but now he realised it was not so. A ferocious will drove him to seek his doom. Feeling that his own death might be near at hand, Felix asked a question that he had long been afraid to utter.

'Herr Trollslayer, what was it you did that you must atone for? What crime drives you to punish yourself so?'

Gotrek looked up to him, then turned his head to gaze off into the night. Felix watched the cable-like muscles of his neck ripple like serpents as he did so.

'If another man asked me that question I would slaughter him. I make allowances for your youth and ignorance and the friendship rite we have undergone. Such a death would make me a kin-slayer. That is a terrible crime. Such crimes we do not talk about.'

Felix had not realised the dwarf was so attached to him. Gotrek looked up at him as if expecting a response.

'I understand,' Felix said.

'Do you, manling? Do you really?' The Trollslayer's voice was as harsh as stones breaking.

Felix smiled ruefully. In that moment he saw the gap that separated man from dwarf. He would never understand their strange taboos, their obsession with oaths and order and pride. He could not see what would drive the Trollslayer to carry out his self-imposed death sentence.

'Your people are too harsh with themselves,' he said.

'Yours are too soft,' the Trollslayer replied. They fell into silence. Both were startled by a quiet, mad laugh. Felix turned, whipping up his blade into the guard position. Gotrek raised his axe.

Out of the mists something shambled. Once it had been a man, Felix decided. The outline was still there. It was as if some mad god held the creature close to a daemonic fire until flesh dripped and ran, then had left it to set in a new and abhorrent form.

'This night we will dance,' it said, in a high-pitched voice that held no hint of sanity. 'Dance and touch.'

It reached out gently to Felix and stroked his arm. Felix recoiled in horror as fingers like clumps of maggots rose towards his face.

'This night at the stone we will dance and touch and rub.' It made as if to embrace him. It smiled, showing short, pointed teeth. Felix stood quietly. He felt like a spectator, distanced from the event that was happening. He pulled back and put the point of his sword against the thing's chest.

'Come no closer,' Felix warned. The thing smiled. Its mouth seemed to grow wider, it showed more small sharp teeth. Its lips rolled back until the bottom half of the face seemed all wet glistening gum and the jaw sank lower like that of a snake. It pushed forward against the sword until beads of blood glistened on its chest. It gave a gurgling, idiotic laugh.

'Dance and touch and rub and eat,' it said, and with inhuman swiftness it writhed around the sword and leapt for Felix.

Swift as it was, the Trollslayer was swifter. In mid-leap his axe caught its neck. The head rolled into the night; a red fountain gushed.

This is not happening, thought Felix.

'What was that? A daemon?' Gotrek asked. Felix could hear the excitement in his voice.

'I think it was once a man,' Felix said. 'One of the tainted ones marked by Chaos. They are abandoned at birth.'

'That one spoke your tongue.'

'Sometimes the taint does not show till they are older. Relatives think they are sick and protect them till they make their way to the woods and vanish.'

'Their kin protect such abominations?'

'It happens. We don't talk about it. It is hard to turn your back on people you love even if they change.'

The dwarf stared at him in disbelief, then shook his head.

'Too soft,' he said. 'Too soft.'

The air was still. Sometimes Felix thought he sensed presences moving in the trees about him and froze nervously, peering into the mist, searching for moving shadows. The encounter with the tainted one had brought home to him the danger of the situation. He felt within him a great fear and a great anger.

Part of the anger was directed at himself for feeling the fear. He was sick and ashamed. He decided that whatever happened he would not repeat his error, standing like a sheep to be slaughtered.

'What was that?' Gotrek asked. Felix looked at him.

'Can't you hear it, manling? Listen! It sounds like chanting.' Felix strained to catch the sound but heard nothing. 'We are close, now. Very close.'

They pushed on in silence. As they trudged through the

mist Gotrek became ever more cautious and left the trail, using the long grass for cover. Felix joined him.

Now he could hear the chanting. It sounded as though it was coming from scores of throats. Some of the voices were human, others were deep and bestial. There were male voices and female voices mingled with the slow beat of a drum, the clash of cymbals and discordant piping.

Felix could make out one word only, repeated over and over until it was driven into his consciousness. The word was 'Slaanesh'.

Felix shuddered. Slaanesh, dark lord of unspeakable pleasures. It was a name that conjured up the worst depths of depravity. It was whispered in the drug dens and vice houses of Altdorf by those so jaded that they sought pleasures beyond human understanding. It was a name associated with corruption and excess and the dark underbelly of Imperial society. For those who followed Slaanesh no stimulation was too bizarre, no pleasure forbidden.

'The mist covers us,' Felix whispered to the Trollslayer.

'Hist! Be quiet. We must get closer.'

They crept forward slowly. The long wet grass dragged at Felix's body, and soon he was damp. Ahead he could see beacons burning in the dark. The scent of blazing wood and cloying sickly-sweet incense filled the air. He looked around, hoping that no latecomer would blunder into them. He felt absurdly exposed.

Inch by inch they advanced. Gotrek dragged his battleaxe along behind him and once Felix touched its sharp blade with his fingers. He cut himself and fought back a desire to scream out.

They reached the edge of the long grass and found themselves staring at a crude ring of six obscenely-shaped stones amid which stood a monolithic slab. The stones glowed greenly with the light of some luminous fungus. On top of each was a brazier which gave off clouds of smoke. Beams of pallid, green moonlight illuminated a hellish scene.

Within the ring danced six humans, masked and garbed in long cloaks. The cloaks were thrown back over one shoulder revealing naked bodies, both male and female. On one hand the revellers each wore finger cymbals which they clashed, in the other they carried switches of birch with which they each lashed the dancer in front.

'Ygrak tu amat Slaanesh!' they cried.

Felix could see that some of the bodies were marked by bruises. The dancers seemed to feel no pain. Perhaps it was the narcotic effect of the incense.

Around the stone ring lolled figures of horror. The drummer was a huge man with the head of a stag and cloven hooves. Near him sat a piper with the head of a dog and hands with suckered fingers. A large crowd of tainted women and men writhed on the ground nearby.

Some of their bodies were subtly distorted: men who were tall with thin, pin heads; short, fat women with three eyes and three breasts. Others were barely recognisable as once having been human. There were scale-covered man-serpents and wolf-headed furred beasts mingling with things that were all teeth and mouth and other orifices. Felix could barely breathe. He watched the entire proceeding with mounting fear.

The drums beat faster, the rhythmic chanting increased in pace, the piping became ever louder and more discordant as the dancers became more frenzied, lashing themselves and their companions until bloody weals became visible. Then there was a clash of cymbals and all fell silent.

Felix thought they had been spotted, and he froze. The smoke of the incense filled his nostrils and seemed to amplify all his senses. He felt even more remote and disconnected from reality. There was a sharp, stabbing pain in his side. He was startled to realise that Gotrek had elbowed him in the ribs. He was pointing to something beyond the stone ring.

Felix struggled to see what loomed in the mist. Then he realised that it was the black coach. In the sudden, shocking silence he heard its door swing open. He held his breath and waited to see what would emerge.

A figure seemed to take shape out of the mist. It was tall and masked, and garbed in layered cloaks of many pastel colours. It moved with calm authority and in its arms it carried something swaddled in brocade cloth. Felix looked at Gotrek but he was watching the unfolding scene with fanatical intensity. Felix wondered if the dwarf had lost his nerve at this late hour.

The newcomer stepped forward into the stone circle.

'Amak tu amat Slaanesh!' it cried, raising its bundle on high. Felix could see that it was a child, though whether living or dead he could not tell.

'Ygrak tu amat Slaanesh! Tzarkol taen amat Slaanesh!' The crowd responded ecstatically.

The cloaked man stared out at the surrounding faces, and it seemed to Felix that the stranger gazed straight at him with calm, brown eyes. He wondered if the coven-master knew they were there and was playing with them.

'Amak tu Slaanesh!' the man cried in a clear voice.

'Amak klessa! Amat Slaanesh!' responded the crowd. It was clear to Felix that some evil ritual had begun. As the rite progressed, the coven-master moved closer to the altar with slow ceremonial steps. Felix felt his mouth go dry. He licked his lips. Gotrek watched the events as if hypnotised.

The child was placed on the altar with a thunderous rumble of drum beats. Now the six dancers each stood beside a pillar, legs astride it, clutching at the stone suggestively. As the ritual progressed they ground themselves against the pillars with slow sinuous movements.

From within his robes the master produced a long wavy-bladed knife. Felix wondered whether the dwarf was going to do something. He could hardly bear to watch.

Slowly the knife was raised, high over the cultist's head. Felix forced himself to look. An ominous presence hovered over the scene. Mist and incense seemed to be clotting together and congealing, and within the cloud Felix thought he could make out a grotesque form writhe and begin to materialise. Felix could bear the tension no longer.

'No!' he shouted.

He and the Trollslayer emerged from the long grass and marched shoulder-to-shoulder towards the stone ring. At first the cultists didn't seem to notice them, but finally the demented drumming stopped and the chanting faded and the cult-master turned to glare at them, astonished.

For a moment everyone stared. No one seemed to understand what was happening. Then the cult-master pointed the knife at them and screamed; 'Kill the interlopers!'

The revellers moved forward in a wave. Felix felt something tug at his leg and then a sharp pain. When he looked down he saw a creature, half woman, half serpent, gnawing at his ankle. He kicked out, pulling his leg free and stabbed down with his sword.

A shock passed up his arm as the blade hit bone. He began to run, following in the wake of Gotrek who was hacking his way towards the altar. The mighty double-bladed axe rose and fell rhythmically and left a trail of red ruin in its path. The cultists seemed drugged and slow to respond but, horrifyingly, they showed no fear. Men and women, tainted and untainted, threw themselves towards the intruders with no thought for their own lives.

Felix hacked and stabbed at anyone who came close. He put his blade under the ribs and into the heart of a dog-faced man who leapt at him. As he tried to tug his blade free a woman with claws and a man with mucous-covered skin leapt on him. Their weight bore him over, knocking the wind from him.

He felt the woman's talons scratch at his face as he put his foot under her stomach and kicked her off. Blood rolled down into his eyes from the cuts. The man had fallen badly, but leapt to grab his throat. Felix fumbled for his dagger with his left hand while he caught the man's throat with his right. The man writhed. He was difficult to grip because of his coating of slime. His own hands tightened inexorably on Felix's throat in return and he rubbed himself against Felix, panting with pleasure.

Blackness threatened to overcome the poet. Little silver points flared before his eyes. He felt an overwhelming urge to relax and fall forward into the darkness. Somewhere far away he heard Gotrek's bellowed war-cry. With an effort of will Felix jerked his dagger clear of its scabbard and plunged it into his assailant's ribs. The creature stiffened and grinned, revealing rows of eel-like teeth. He gave an ecstatic moan even as he died.

'Slaanesh, take me,' the man shrieked. 'Ah, the pain, the lovely pain!'

Felix pulled himself to his feet just as the clawed woman

rose to hers. He lashed out with his boot, connected with her jaw. There was a crunch, and she fell backwards. Felix shook his head to clear the blood from his eyes.

The majority of the cultists had concentrated on Gotrek. This had kept Felix alive. The dwarf was trying to hack his way towards the heart of the stone circle. Even as he moved, the press of bodies against him slowed him down. Felix could see that he bled from dozens of small cuts.

The ferocious energy of the dwarf was terrible to see. He frothed at the mouth and ranted as he chopped, sending limbs and heads everywhere. He was covered in a filthy matting of gore, but in spite of his sheer ferocity Felix could tell the fight was going against Gotrek. Even as he watched, a cloaked reveller hit the dwarf with a club and Gotrek went down under a wave of bodies. So he has met his doom, thought Felix, just as he desired.

Beyond the ruck of the melee, the cult-master had regained his composure. Once more he began to chant, and raised the dagger on high. The terrible shape that had been forming from the mist seemed once again to coalesce.

Felix had a premonition that if it took on full substance they were doomed. He could not fight his way through the bodies that surrounded the Trollslayer. For a long moment he watched the curve-bladed knife reflecting the Morrslieb light.

Then he drew back his own dagger. 'Sigmar guide my hand,' he prayed and threw. The blade flew straight and true to the throat of the High Priest, hitting beneath the mask where flesh was exposed. With a gurgle, the cult-master toppled backwards.

A long whine of frustration filled the air and the mist seemed to evaporate. The shape within the mist vanished. As one, the cultists looked up in shock. The tainted ones turned to stare at him. Felix found himself confronted by the mad glare of dozens of unfriendly eyes. He stood immobile and very, very afraid. The silence was deathly.

Then there was an almighty roar and Gotrek emerged from amidst the pile of bodies, pummelling about him with ham-sized fists. He reached down and from somewhere retrieved his axe. He shortened his grip on the haft and laid about him with its shaft. Felix scooped up his own sword and ran to join him. They fought through the crush until they were back to back.

The cultists, filled with fear at the loss of their leader, began to flee into the night and mist. Soon Felix and Gotrek stood alone under the shadows of the Darkstone Ring.

Gotrek looked at Felix balefully, blood clotted in his crested hair. In the witch-light he looked daemonic. 'I am robbed of a mighty death, manling.'

He raised his axe menacingly. Felix wondered if he were still berserk and about to chop him down in spite of their binding oath. Gotrek began to advance slowly towards him. Then the dwarf grinned. 'It would seem the gods preserve me for a greater doom yet.'

He planted his axe hilt first into the ground and began to laugh until the tears ran down his face. Having exhausted his laughter, he turned to the altar and picked up the infant. 'It lives,' he said.

Felix began to inspect the corpses of the cloaked cultists. He unmasked them. The first one was a blonde-haired girl covered in weals and bruises. The second was a young man. He had an amulet in the shape of a hammer hanging almost mockingly round his neck.

'I don't think we'll be going back to the inn,' Felix said sadly.

* * *

One local tale tells of an infant found on the steps of the temple of Shallya in Hartzroch. It was wrapped in a blood-soaked cloak of Sudenland wool, a pouch of gold lay nearby, and a steel amulet in the shape of a hammer was round its neck. The priestess swore she saw a black coach thundering away in the dawn light.

The natives of Hartzroch tell another and darker tale of how Ingrid Hauptmann and Gunter, the innkeeper's son, were slain in some horrific sacrifice to the Dark Powers. The road wardens who found the corpses up by the Darkstone Ring agreed it must have been a terrible rite. The bodies looked as if they had been chopped up with an axe wielded by a daemon.

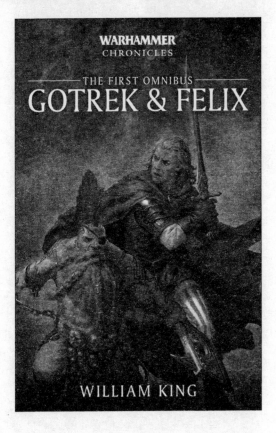

WARHAMMER
ADVENTURES
STORIES FROM THE FAR FUTURE

WARPED GALAXIES

ATTACK OF THE NECRON

CAVAN SCOTT

CHAPTER ONE

INTRUDERS

Zelia Lor awoke to the sound of buzzing in her cabin. She groaned. What time was it? Her bunk creaked as she turned over, pulling her thick woollen blanket with her. Surely that couldn't be the alarm already? The shrill drone continued, flitting to and fro near the ceiling. Zelia pulled the blanket over her head, but the noise persisted. Throwing back the covers, she peered up into the gloom.

That was no alarm. There was something up there, darting back and forth.

'Hello?' Zelia called out, her voice croaking from lack of sleep. She'd been up late last night, helping her mum catalogue artefacts in the ship's cargo bay.

A series of high-pitched chirps and whistles came from somewhere near the ceiling. Zelia reached out, feeling for the luminator switch next to her bunk. Glow-globes flickered into life, the tiny invader squealing in surprise as it was bathed in sudden light.

Zelia frowned as her eyes focused on her flighty visitor. It was a servo-sprite, one of the small winged robots that her mother used on board their planet-hopper, the *Scriptor*. The whimsical little things had been created by her mother's assistant, Mekki. They had tiny bronze bodies and spindly limbs, with probes and data-connectors for fingers and toes. Their heads were long, with wide optical-beads for eyes that gave the little automata a constant look of surprise. Mesh wings whirred on the robot's back, producing the strident buzz that had woken Zelia.

'What are you doing up there?' Zelia asked, rubbing sleep from her eyes.

The servo-sprite chattered nervously at itself. If Zelia didn't know better she would have thought the thing was agitated, but like all the robots her mother used on their expeditions servo-sprites were just machines. Elise Lor was an explorator, a scholar who travelled the length and breadth of the Imperium excavating technology from years gone by, and who often dreamed of digging up artefacts from the Dark Age of Technology, that period thousands of years ago when machines thought for themselves. Those days were long gone. Like so many things in the 41st millennium, artificial intelligence was a heresy, prohibited by order of the Eternal Emperor himself. While Mekki's creations sometimes acted as if they were alive, they were just following their programming. They were tools, nothing more. However, something must have spooked the little automaton for it to squeeze through the gap beneath her cabin door. Gooseflesh crawled over Zelia's skin. Why would a servo-sprite hide? Something was wrong.

Swinging her legs off the bunk, Zelia gasped as her bare feet touched the cold metal deck. The floors of the *Scriptor* were supposed to be heated, but like most of the systems on the ramshackle spaceship, the heating hadn't worked properly for months. The planet-hopper was old – very old – and its systems often failed faster than Mekki could fix them. But for all its glitches, the *Scriptor* had been Zelia's home since she was born. She knew every creak of the hull, every bleep of the central cogitator. The low thrum of the engines lulled her to sleep every night. They were a comfort, especially during long journeys across the Imperium, rocketing from one dig to another. It was an odd, topsy-turvy life, helping her mum uncover crashed spaceships or ancient machines on distant worlds all across the galaxy, but Zelia wouldn't have it any other way.

But now, the *Scriptor* didn't feel comforting. It felt uneasy, and Zelia had no idea why. Pulling on her jacket and bandolier, Zelia tapped the vox stitched into her sleeve. The communicator beeped, opening a channel to the flight deck.

'Mum? Are you there?'

There was no reply, neither from mum, nor Lexmechanic Erasmus, her mother's archaeological partner and an expert in galactic languages, both ancient and alien. There was no point trying to contact Mekki. Her mum's young assistant was a whizz with technology, but hardly ever spoke to Zelia, even though they were around the same age. At twelve, she was a full year older than Mekki was, but they were largely strangers, the Martian boy preferring the company of his machines. Zelia didn't mind. If she was honest, Mekki made her a little uncomfortable. He was so intense, with his pale skin and cold grey eyes.

Still, he would know what to do with a flustered servo-sprite.

The robot bumbled around her head as she opened the cabin door. She swatted it away, but it stayed close as she stepped out into the corridor. The passageway was quiet, electro-candles spluttering along the creaky walls.

The door to her mum's cabin was ajar, and Zelia could see it was empty. For a woman who spent her life cataloguing artefacts, Elise Lor was incredibly untidy. Curios from her travels were crammed into nooks and crannies, while towers of textbooks and battered data-slates teetered on every available surface. Elise's library was spread throughout the ship, piled high along the narrow gantries. How mum ever found anything was a mystery, and yet she always seemed to be able to put her finger on any text at a moment's notice.

But where was she now? Zelia crept down the corridor, checking Erasmus's cabin, but the elderly scholar was nowhere to be seen. He wasn't in his room or on the mess deck where the *Scriptor*'s crew gathered to eat. Zelia checked the chrono-display on her vox. It was early, barely sunrise. Had mum and Erasmus gone to the dig already?

Zelia jumped at a noise from the back of the ship. Something heavy had been dropped, the deep clang echoing around the planet-hopper. That had to have come from the cargo bay, where Elise stored their most valuable discoveries. They had been on this planet, a remote hive world called Targian, for three months now, and the hold was brimming with ancient tech. Of course, the noise could just have been Mekki, checking through the previous day's finds, but somehow, she knew it wasn't. Mekki was a lot of things, but clumsy wasn't one of them. He would never drop something if he could help it. As the servo-sprite fussed around her head, Zelia picked up a heavy-looking ladle that Elise had used to slop grox stew into their bowls the night before. It wasn't much of a defence, but it would have to do.

Zelia inched towards the cargo bay, praying that she'd

find Mekki on the other side of the hold's heavy doors. She paused, listening through the thick metal. There was a flurry of movement on the other side of the door, the scrape of leather against deck-plates, and then silence. Trying to ignore the increasingly frantic buzzing of the servo-sprite, Zelia stepped forwards and the doors wheezed open.

'Hello? Mekki, are you in here?'

There was no answer. The cargo bay was silent, the lights kept permanently low to protect the more valuable artefacts. She crept through the collection, tall cabinets on either side.

Something moved ahead. Her grip tightened on the ladle.

'Mekki? Seriously, this isn't funny.'

A boot crunched behind her. Zelia whirled around, swinging the ladle.

'You need to be careful,' a gruff voice said. 'You could hurt someone with that!'

Zelia cried out as thick fingers caught her wrist. They squeezed, and the metal spoon clattered to the floor.

'That's better.'

A stranger loomed over her, muscles bunched beneath a scruffy vest festooned with brightly coloured patches. His hair was styled into a lurid green mohawk, a tattoo of a large red cat leaping over his left ear. It was a Runak – a ferocious scavenger native to Targian with jagged scales instead of fur. Zelia had only seen the creatures out on the plains, but imagined they smelled better than the thug who was threatening her in her own home.

'Let go of me,' Zelia cried out, trying to pull away.

'I don't think so, Ladle-Girl,' the tattooed thug leered, before calling over his shoulder. 'You can come out. It's only a little brat.'

Brat? The thug must only have been a year or two older

than Zelia. He was strong though. There was no way of breaking his grip. More strangers slipped out of the shadow – two boys, and a girl with spiked purple hair and a glowing eye-implant. They all wore similar patches on their jackets, obviously members of the same gang.

'What do you want?' Zelia squeaked, and her captor smiled, showing uneven, stained teeth.

'That's a good question.' The thug glanced around, his small, cruel eyes scanning the rusting relics on the shelves. 'We thought this place would be full of treasure, didn't we, Talen?'

The ganger behind him nodded. This one wasn't as big, but still looked like he could handle himself in a fight. His blond hair was cropped short at the sides and a small scar ran through one of his thick, dark eyebrows. He held no weapons in his gloved hands, but Zelia couldn't help but notice the snub-nosed beamer hanging next to the leather pouch on his belt.

'That's what you told us, Rizz, but it looks like a load of old junk to me.'

'Yeah, old junk,' Rizz parroted, pulling Zelia closer. 'Where's the real booty? Where've you stashed it?'

'This is all we have,' Zelia told him, glancing down at the hefty weapon Rizz held in his free hand. The ganger had fashioned a mace out of a long girder topped with a blunt slab of corroded metal.

'You like my spud-jacker?' Rizz said, brandishing the make-shift weapon. 'I call her Splitter. Do you want to know why?'

'I think I can guess,' Zelia replied.

"Cos, I split skulls with her,' he said anyway, as if she were the idiot, not him. 'Ain't that right, Talen?'

The blond-haired juve shifted uncomfortably, glancing

nervously at the cargo bay doors. 'We should go, Rizz. There's nothing here.'

Rizz glared at the younger kid. 'Oi. I give the orders. Not you.'

'Then order us to get out of here. We're wasting our time.'

Rizz swung around, nearly pulling Zelia off her feet.

'I'll waste you in a minute,' he growled, brandishing Splitter menacingly.

Zelia saw her chance and took it. She lashed out with her foot, kicking Rizz's shin.

'Ow!' he yelped, spinning her around so she crashed into the nearest cabinet, cogs and gears tumbling all around her. Zelia snatched a length of metal piping from the floor, but a swipe of the spud-jacker sent it flying across the cargo bay.

'Nice try,' Rizz sneered above her. 'But I'm not going to ask you again. Where's the valuable stuff? Where are you hiding it?'

'I told you,' she shouted back, gripping her aching fingers. 'This is all there is.'

'Liar,' Rizz bellowed, raising the spud-jacker high above his head. 'Splitter hates liars, and so do I.'

With a feral roar, he brought the mace crashing down.

YOUR
NEXT READ

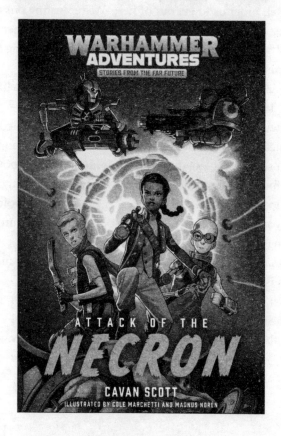

ATTACK OF THE NECRON
by Cavan Scott

A new adventure begins in the far future! When her world is attacked by Necrons, Zelia Lor and a rag-tag group of survivors must fight to escape and reach the mysterious Emperor's Seat.

CITY OF
LIFESTONE

TOM HUDDLESTON

CHAPTER ONE

THE SILENT MARKET

The direwolf's jaws snapped and Kiri threw herself sideways, tumbling into a rocky ravine. Thorny bushes snagged at her cloak as she picked herself up, loading her catapult. The wolf bounded alongside, its shaggy black mane outlined against the tall trees and the pale sky. Up ahead she could see her travelling companion, Harvin, casting a panicked look back as he fled, his pedlar's pack clanking with copper pots and iron tools.

Then the wolf darted closer, paws scrabbling on the edge of the ravine, preparing to spring. Kiri loosed her shot, and to her satisfaction it struck the creature square on the snout. The direwolf whined, sprawling in the dirt. Kiri put on a burst of speed, hearing the creature scrabble to its feet and continue the pursuit.

They'd been running since dawn. A fallen bridge had delayed them the day before, forcing them to camp in the forest. Kiri had been woken by strange sounds and a smell of decay, the air so cold she could see her breath. Then the direwolf had attacked, bounding from the darkness, threatening to drag Harvin away until a shot from Kiri's catapult drove it back. They hadn't had a moment to rest since.

But in truth, Kiri reflected, she'd been running for the better part of a year. Yes, the Realmgate had brought her to Ghyran, just as she'd hoped. But that had been her last stroke of luck – from then on, every day had been fight or flight. The Realm of Life was rightly named, every corner of it overrun with living things. The trouble was, most of them wanted to eat her. She'd battled packs of gryph-hounds in the Nevergreen Mountains and had spent two nights trapped in the nest of a long-tailed cockatrice, a meal for its caterwauling fledglings. And the towns weren't much better: the street gangs in the great city of Hammerhal were as dangerous as any wolfpack.

She glanced back, expecting the direwolf to be hard behind them. But to her surprise the animal had fallen back, sitting on its haunches and narrowing its yellow eyes. Kiri slowed her pace, tugging on Harvin's sleeve.

'What's it doing?' she hissed. 'Waiting for reinforcements?'

The pedlar shook his head. 'I told you we'd be safe if we made it to Lifestone – those hairy fiends won't go near the place. And here we are. Look.'

He pointed and Kiri raised her eyes, tugging back her grey headscarf. A wide valley fell ahead, the trees replaced by slopes of scrub-grass and stony soil. Beyond was a wall of dark mountains, rising peak upon jagged peak to the limits of her vision. But closer, at the valley's head, was a sprawling shadow, a darkness that couldn't be natural.

A city. Lifestone.

Kiri's heart tightened. This couldn't be the place her mother had sent her to find – the city was wreathed in mist and shadow, a flock of noisy ravens circling overhead. Rain began to fall, a thin drizzle that somehow made her feel even more sweaty and uncomfortable.

'Are you sure this is right?' she asked. 'I mean, absolutely sure?'

Harvin smiled, displaying his last remaining teeth. She'd met him on the road six days before, and he'd offered his guidance. He was a decent sort – a little slow-witted, perhaps, but generous with his supplies.

'I've been peddling up and down this road all my born days. You think I don't know where I'm going?'

'But Lifestone is a place of healing,' Kiri insisted, recalling her mother's words. 'There are gardens, and orchards and sparkling fountains. There's… life!'

Harvin shrugged. 'Once upon a time, maybe. When I was young they said this was the place to go if you had wounds that wouldn't heal, and not just on the outside if you know what I mean. You had to walk a hard road to find it, but it was worth the effort.'

'So what happened?' Kiri asked.

Harvin shrugged, hitching up his trousers. 'I dunno. The crops went bad, I s'pose. People moved away. This is how it's been for as long as I remember. Sorry it's not what you was expecting.'

Kiri tightened her fists until her knuckles turned white. Somewhere deep down she'd known it would be this way, that the city Chetan spoke of was just a figment of her imagination. Years of servitude had twisted her mother's mind – who could blame her for retreating into some half-dreamed vision of the past?

That didn't make it any easier, though. Because buried

beneath all those doubts and fears, Kiri had also carried a little flame of hope. Hope that her mother's words would prove true, hope that she would find Lifestone and all her hardships would be over.

That flame had just flickered out.

They drew closer, and now she could make out individual buildings – wooden shacks nestled together in the crook of the valley, with larger, more ornate structures of hewn grey stone on the higher slopes. But even these once mighty manses looked battered and worn down – she saw fallen arches and crumbling spires, their jagged tops like dogs' teeth biting at the sky. At the top of the rise was a structure paler than the rest, a huge white palace of towers and parapets, all centred around a coloured glass dome that sparkled in the light. But even this was falling into disrepair, its walls shrouded with vines, its minarets crumbling.

Ruined buildings were commonplace in Ghyran, of course; centuries of war had left even mighty Hammerhal in pieces. But this was different somehow – she didn't see any scorch marks or cannon-holes, no signs of battle or siege. The place seemed to have simply fallen apart, and no one had bothered to repair it.

Kiri gritted her teeth, fighting down a wave of despair. She was strong, she told herself, stronger than she'd ever been. Life in the slave camp had toughened her body, while a year in the wilderness had done the same for her mind. The reason for this disappointment was because she'd let herself hope in the first place. But that hope was gone now; it couldn't hurt her any more. She would become as hard and unbending as life itself.

The outer wall of Lifestone rose above them, ravens crowing from the battlements. This at least seemed intact, a sturdy fortification of granite boulders so huge it must've taken a team of rhinox to haul them. The road led through an arch beneath a raised portcullis, and the two of them followed.

Harvin nodded to the Freeguild soldier minding the gate, a scruffy slob in a tatty black uniform with the faded symbol of a fountain stitched on the breast. He didn't respond, picking his teeth with the point of his dagger. They passed into a massive courtyard, and Kiri stopped dead in surprise. The space was packed with stalls and busy with people, but all she heard was silence.

She'd been to markets all across the realm – they were good places to pick up work and news and, if she was desperate, to steal a bite to eat. But from the vast covered pavilions of Hammerhal to the tiniest village fayre they each had one thing in common – noise. Traders' cries, furious haggling, angry curses and joyful greetings, these were the lifeblood of any Ghyran bazaar.

Except, apparently, this one. Figures moved from stall to stall, selecting goods and handing over their coins; she saw men and women, children and old folk, their faces stern and joyless as they heaped their baskets with grain and root vegetables, hard bread and eggs the size of Kiri's head. A sign above a herbalist's stall read 'Put the Spring Back in your Step with Archimband's Amazing Unguent!', but the words were faded and the owner looked as miserable as everyone else.

Hinges creaked ominously and Kiri saw a sign outside an old tavern: 'The Fountain', it read, clearly a popular symbol in these parts. She peered through the inn's filthy windows and saw men at the bar, perched on high stools in total silence. A rough-looking gang of stout, short-legged Duardin sat in the shadows of an alcove, smoking long pipes and staring sullenly into their stone tankards. She wondered if there were any Aelf-folk in Lifestone, but it seemed unlikely – the Wanderers were surely too proud to show their faces in a dump like this.

Harvin led her across the courtyard to a stall selling cookware, where a burly young man peered at them from below a dull green awning. 'Expected you yesterday,' he grunted as Harvin began to unpack, lining his wares up on the counter.

'We hit trouble on the road,' he said. 'Had to spend the night in the Stonewoods.'

The stallholder frowned, his bushy eyebrows meeting in the middle. 'You don't want to do that. There's been stories.'

'What sort of stories?' Kiri asked.

He scowled down at her. 'Who are you meant to be?'

'That's Kiri,' Harvin said. 'I showed her the way here.'

'Why would anyone want to come here?' the stallholder sneered. 'Anyhow, Lord Elias sent a party of his best Freeguild soldiers into the Stonewoods last month, hunting Tuskers for his table. They never came back.'

Harvin's eyes widened. 'I thought I heard something in the trees last night. Didn't you, Kiri?'

'There's been other tales too,' the young man went on, gesturing up the hill. 'Giant rats up near the old theatre, walking on their hind legs and wearing clothes. Skaven, they say.'

'Skaven?' Harvin snorted. 'They're just a kids' story.'

The young man shrugged. 'Just telling you what I heard.'

'What happened here?' Kiri asked, unable to hold her tongue any longer. 'Where are the orchards and the gardens? Where are the houses of healing? And why is everything so *quiet*?'

'I don't know what you're on about,' the young man snapped. 'This is Lifestone – this is how it's always been. Now go away, I'm not buying.' He thrust Harvin's goods off his counter and dropped the awning.

The pedlar turned to Kiri apologetically. 'Brodwin's never been friendly, but that's rude even for him.'

She looked around. 'I thought Ghyran was the Lady Alarielle's realm, the Realm of Life. But this place is about as lively as a mortuary. You said it used to be different, so what changed?'

Harvin shook his head, then he pointed up between the narrow buildings. 'There's a Sigmarite temple about three streets thataway. They always used to have a bed and broth for a weary traveller, and they might have some answers for you, too.'

Kiri nodded. 'Thank you. For everything. You're the first person in a long time who's actually been kind to me.' Harvin smiled and she grinned back. Then she remembered what she'd decided about being hard and unbending and straightened her face.

She weaved through the shuffling market crowds, the silence weighing her down. She saw a butcher carving up a rhinox carcass, hacking at it glumly with a blunt cleaver. A horse surprised her and she jumped, backing into a man hauling three baskets of wheat. He glared, gathering up his load and moving on. *It's all wrong,* she thought. *He should've yelled at me and made a scene.* She'd have been happier if he had.

The rough buildings rose above her as she headed for the street Harvin had gestured to. The rain was falling harder now, drumming on the canvas stalls and wooden roofs.

Then a soft voice said, 'Girl,' and Kiri turned. A lady in black stood beneath the awning of an apothecary's shop, crystal flasks and copper alembics gleaming in the window. Her face was half-hidden beneath a fur-lined hood and her elegant black robe was finely stitched with silken thread. She beckoned and Kiri joined her beneath the awning.

'Share my shelter, child.' The lady smiled through pale lips. Then she gestured subtly towards the courtyard. 'I wonder, did you know you're being watched?'

Kiri looked up in time to see a man in the crowd turning away, his head wreathed in smoke from a curved arkenwood pipe. He was tall and thin, with greying hair almost to his shoulders. He wore a black hat with a wide brim and carried a wooden staff.

'He's been following you,' the hooded lady said. 'Around here folks call him the Shadowcaster, though Child Snatcher would be a better name, if you ask me. He takes children, they say, and carries them off to that big palace on the hill.'

Kiri felt her pulse quicken. The man didn't glance back, stalking away through the market, his staff tapping on the cobbles. He was soon lost in the crowd.

'Perhaps you should go,' the hooded lady whispered. 'Now, while he's not looking.'

'Thank you,' Kiri said gratefully. Then she ducked into the rainswept streets and ran.

YOUR
NEXT READ

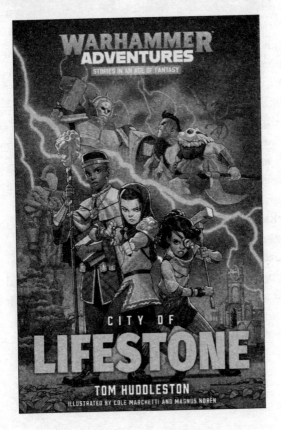

CITY OF LIFESTONE
by Tom Huddleston

Far from home and freed from slavery, Kiri embarks on an epic adventure across the Mortal Realms, accompanied by a group of special friends. But dark forces gather to stop them…

ABOUT THE AUTHORS

Dan Abnett has written over fifty novels, including *Anarch*, the latest instalment in the acclaimed Gaunt's Ghosts series. He has also written the Ravenor and Eisenhorn books, the most recent of which is *The Magos*. For the Horus Heresy, he is the author of the Siege of Terra novel *Saturnine*, as well as *Horus Rising*, *Legion*, *The Unremembered Empire*, *Know No Fear* and *Prospero Burns*, the last two of which were both *New York Times* bestsellers. He also scripted *Macragge's Honour*, the first Horus Heresy graphic novel, as well as numerous Black Library audio dramas. Many of his short stories have been collected into the volume *Lord of the Dark Millennium*. He lives and works in Maidstone, Kent.

Guy Haley is the author of the Siege of Terra novel *The Lost and the Damned*, as well as the Horus Heresy novels *Titandeath*, *Wolfsbane* and *Pharos*, and the Primarchs novels *Konrad Curze: The Night Haunter*, *Corax: Lord of Shadows* and *Perturabo: The Hammer of Olympia*. He has also written many Warhammer 40,000 novels, including the first book in the Dawn of Fire series, *Avenging Son*, as well as *Belisarius Cawl: The Great Work*, *Dark Imperium*, *Dark Imperium: Plague War*, *The Devastation of Baal*, *Dante*, *Darkness in the Blood* and *Astorath: Angel of Mercy*. He has also written stories set in the Age of Sigmar, included in *War Storm*, *Ghal Maraz* and *Call of Archaon*. He lives in Yorkshire with his wife and son.

Rachel Harrison is the author of the Warhammer 40,000 novel *Honourbound*, featuring the character Commissar Severina Raine, as well the accompanying short stories 'Execution', 'Trials', 'Fire and Thunder', 'A Company of Shadows', and 'The Darkling Hours', which won a 2019 Scribe Award in the Best Short Story category. Also for Warhammer 40,000 she has written the novel *Mark of Faith*, the novella *Blood Rite*, numerous short stories including 'The Third War' and 'Dishonoured', the short story 'Dirty Dealings' for Necromunda, and the Warhammer Horror audio drama *The Way Out*.

Tom Huddleston is the author of the Warhammer Adventures: Realm Quest series, and has also written three instalments in the Star Wars: Adventures in Wild Space saga. His other works include the futuristic fantasy adventure story *FloodWorld* and its upcoming sequel, *DustRoad*. He lives in East London.

William King is the author of the Tyrion and Teclis saga and the Macharian Crusade trilogy, as well as the much-loved Gotrek & Felix series and the Space Wolf novels. His short stories have appeared in many magazines and compilations, including *White Dwarf* and *Inferno!*. Bill was born in Stranraer, Scotland, in 1959 and currently lives in Prague.

Sandy Mitchell is the author of a long-running series of Warhammer 40,000 novels about the Hero of the Imperium, Commissar Ciaphas Cain, as well as the audio drama *Dead In The Water*. He has also written a plethora of short stories, including 'The Last Man' in the *Sabbat Worlds* anthology, along with several novels set in the Warhammer World. He lives and works in Cambridge.

Thomas Parrott is the kind of person who reads RPG rule books for fun. He fell in love with Warhammer 40,000 when he was fifteen and read the short story 'Apothecary's Honour' in the *Dark Imperium* anthology, and has never looked back. 'Spiritus In Machina' was his first story for Black Library, and he has since written 'Salvage Rites', 'Fates and Fortunes' and the novella *Isha's Lament*.

Josh Reynolds' extensive Black Library back catalogue includes the Horus Heresy Primarchs novel *Fulgrim: The Palatine Phoenix*, and three Horus Heresy audio dramas featuring the Blackshields. His Warhammer 40,000 work includes the Space Marine Conquests novel *Apocalypse, Lukas the Trickster* and the Fabius Bile novels. He has written many stories set in the Age of Sigmar, including the novels *Shadespire: The Mirrored City, Soul Wars, Eight Lamentations: Spear of Shadows*, the Hallowed Knights novels *Plague Garden* and *Black Pyramid*, and *Nagash: The Undying King*. He has written the Warhammer Horror novel *Dark Harvest*, and novella 'The Beast in the Trenches', featured in the portmanteau novel *The Wicked and the Damned*. He has recently penned the Necromunda novel *Kal Jerico: Sinner's Bounty*. He lives and works in Sheffield.

Cavan Scott has written for such popular franchises as Star Wars, Doctor Who, Judge Dredd. LEGO DC Super Heroes, Penguins of Madagascar, Adventure Time and many, many more. The writer of a number of novellas and short stories set within the Warhammer 40,000 universe, including the Warhammer Adventures: Warped Galaxies series, Cavan became a UK number one bestseller with his 2016 World Book Day title, *Star Wars: Adventures in Wild Space – The Escape*.

Gav Thorpe is the author of the Horus Heresy novels *The First Wall*, *Deliverance Lost*, *Angels of Caliban* and *Corax*, as well as the novella *The Lion*, which formed part of the *New York Times* bestselling collection *The Primarchs*, and several audio dramas. He has written many novels for Warhammer 40,000, including *Ashes of Prospero*, *Imperator: Wrath of the Omnissiah* and the Rise of the Ynnari novels *Ghost Warrior* and *Wild Rider*. He also wrote the *Path of the Eldar* and *Legacy of Caliban* trilogies, and two volumes in The Beast Arises series. For Warhammer, Gav has penned the End Times novel *The Curse of Khaine*, the Warhammer Chronicles omnibus *The Sundering*, and recently wrote the Age of Sigmar novel *The Red Feast*. In 2017, Gav won the David Gemmell Legend Award for his Age of Sigmar novel *Warbeast*. He lives and works in Nottingham.

Chris Wraight is the author of the Horus Heresy novels Scars and *The Path of Heaven*, the Primarchs novels *Leman Russ: The Great Wolf* and *Jaghatai Khan: Warhawk of Chogoris*, the novellas *Brotherhood of the Storm, Wolf King* and *Valdor: Birth of the Imperium*, and the audio drama *The Sigillite*. For Warhammer 40,000 he has written *The Lords of Silence, Vaults of Terra: The Carrion Throne, Vaults of Terra: The Hollow Mountain, Watchers of the Throne: The Emperor's Legion*, the Space Wolves novels *Blood of Asaheim* and *Stormcaller*, and many more. Additionally, he has many Warhammer novels to his name, including the Warhammer Chronicles novel *Master of Dragons*, which forms part of the War of Vengeance series. Chris lives and works in Bradford-on-Avon, in south-west England.

C L Werner's Black Library credits include the Age of Sigmar novels *Overlords of the Iron Dragon*, *Profit's Ruin*, *The Tainted Heart* and *Beastgrave*, the novella 'Scion of the Storm' in *Hammers of Sigmar*, and the Warhammer Horror novel *Castle of Blood*. For Warhammer he has written the novels *Deathblade*, *Mathias Thulmann: Witch Hunter*, *Runefang* and *Brunner the Bounty Hunter*, the Thanquol and Boneripper series and Warhammer Chronicles: The Black Plague series. For Warhammer 40,000 he has written the Space Marine Battles novel *The Siege of Castellax*. Currently living in the American south-west, he continues to write stories of mayhem and madness set in the Warhammer worlds.